Azrael Series

Short Story Compilation

AYSE HAFIZA

AYSE HAFIZA

Copyright © 2012 AYSE HAFIZA

All rights reserved.

ISBN-13: 978-1530900053
ISBN-10: 1530900050

Dedicated to those who remember death often.

Connect and sign up to receive a free ebook.

www.aysehafiza.co.uk

Connect on Twitter: @aysehafiza

Connect on Facebook: Facebook.com/aysehafiza

1	The Afterlife of Abdul	1
1.1	Abdul	2
1.2	Jenny	12
1.3	Sophie	16
1.4	Azrael	24
2	King Solomon and the Cat	26
2.1	Protecting Graves	27
2.2	The Lesson	33
2.3	The Merchant	37
2.4	The Hoopoe	41
2.5	Bilkis the Queen of Sheba	44
3	Mr. Time	48
3.1	The Countdown	49
3.2	The Dream	53
3.3	Azrael	59
3.4	Forgiveness	66
3.5	The End	72
4	About the Author	76
5	Additional titles from Ayse Hafiza	77
6	Disclaimer	78

The Afterlife of Abdul

Azrael Series Book 1

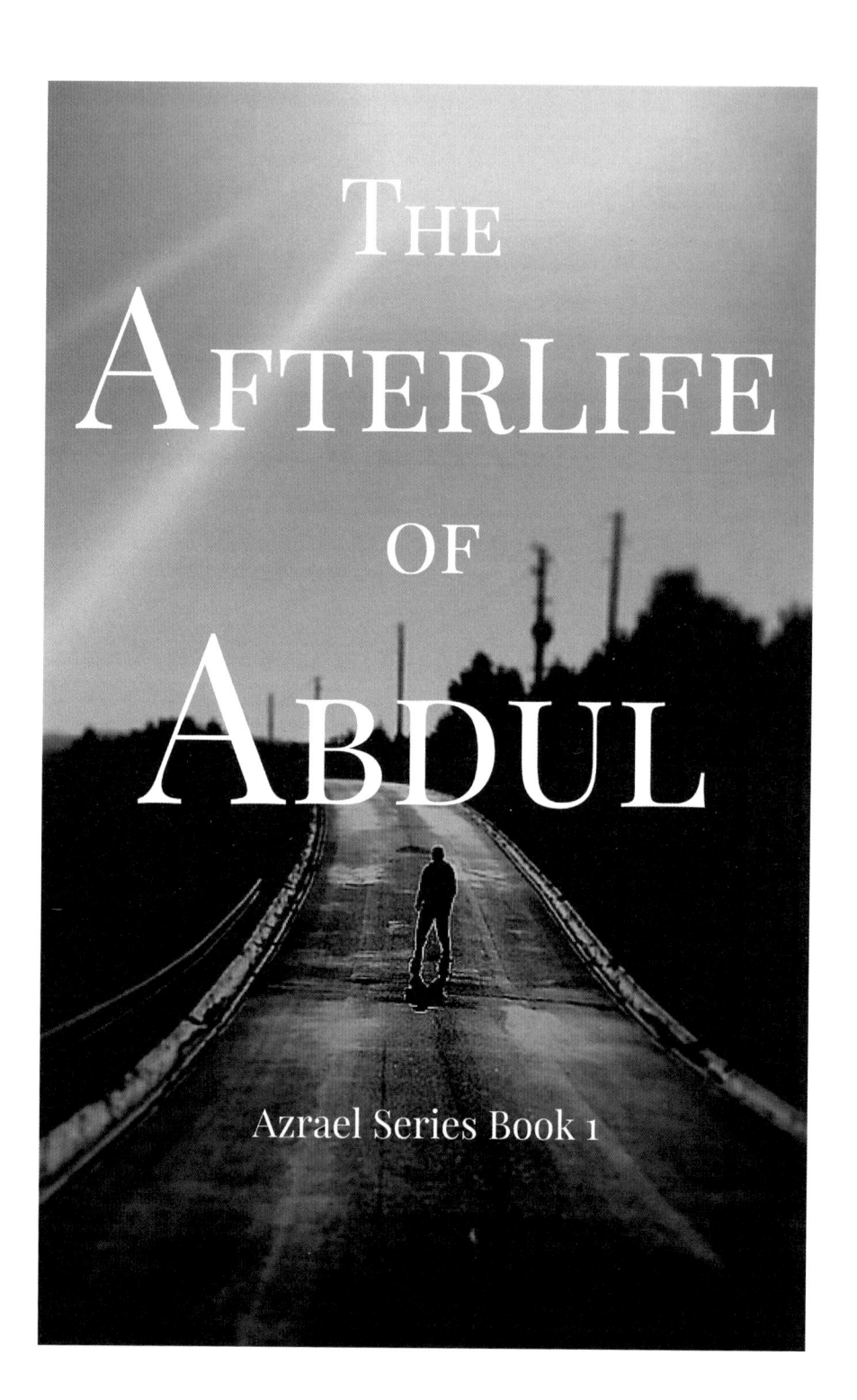

1.1 ABDUL

The relentless wind and rain whip past my torso. Water vapor from the road forms droplets on the visor of my helmet; they blur my vision, but driving faster is the remedy. Small streams form pathways as my speed increases, moving the raindrops to the sides of my helmet, which helps me see clearly. I grip the handlebars tighter. My shoulders lock in position to create a frame—my bike and body are one on the road. The wet winds envelop me as the familiar seasonal chill sinks into my bones. The phosphorus orange street lamps pass by, faster and faster, their eerie orange light reflecting on the varying shades of gray belonging to hard concrete and parked cars. London has hard lines, and tonight it has a hostile feeling. The intermittent light from the lampposts on the sides of the roads reminds me of my childhood, when I used to try and count them from the warmth of the backseat of Dad's car. Being on my motorbike is a stark contrast to that cozy and comforting memory. I try to hold onto that thought as it warms my heart and gives me respite from the cold.

Encouraged by this thought, I remind myself of the blessings I have in my life, and what I should be grateful for. Immediately my motorbike leathers come to mind. This second skin protects me from the elements. I mentally repeat the mantra I set for my journey, 'Thank God for my leathers.'

I think about these words as my motorbike's front wheel hungrily devours the wet road in front of me. The din from the exhaust accompanies every rev of the handlebars. I am freezing my ass off to get to North London, and even with no traffic my journey is another twenty minutes.

Breaking the silence, the voice in my head says, "Forget about being grateful!" Almost dictatorial in its tone, it asks, "Why did I leave home?"

I know the answer before the question ends.

"I let her talk me into coming out tonight," I silently answer. I had prepared justifications as to why I was driving to North London on a night like this, trying to prevent an internal argument with the voice in my head.

The Pakistani in me says, "To be honest, I would rather spend the evening at home with the family, digesting Mum's delicious home cooked lamb." I had eaten the lamb too quickly to savor, and my dinner sits in the bottom of my gut, making me uncomfortable. Eating fast meant I could leave the house sooner. I think about how on a Friday night like this, I am normally relaxing in front of the TV, watching a film or a talk show to wind down from the hectic week, which had passed too quickly. A warm cup of tea in my right hand and a chocolate bar in the left, comfortable and cozy with my feet curled up on the sofa, watching TV celebrities being quizzed. I picture myself with my favorite socks on and my fleece blanket on my lap. The image in my mind makes me feel warm and brings a smile to my face even though here I am, on my motorbike in the freezing cold, driving fast for the road conditions in a rush to get to Mona's house.

The voice asks, "Why do you give Mona this level of importance?"

My internal justification answers in a reasonable tone, "Sure, ok, I like her, and I have dreams too. Like everyone else my age. I'm twenty-six, and as a young man, a young Muslim man, I know I want a family. That starts with getting married. I want the security of a family life, an unshakable family life. My parents have it, and it's normal in my culture for a guy my age to be thinking about his future. My uncles and aunties have been asking my parents questions about my plans, and I know it's time to make something happen for myself. I'm not sure how much culture has to do with it because even the boys at work, from all different cultures and backgrounds, have girlfriends, some have boyfriends, and some have wives. We all watch movies and read the news, so we know that love is not easy. Some of my friends have it rough because they married quickly and divorced quickly too. No, sir! That is not for me. I don't want that, and I don't want a girlfriend for years and years, either. I want to move ahead with a woman that I can see a future with, that I can build something with."

Trying to get to Mona tonight is about an investment in my dreams and my future. Our relationship is in its early days, but I know I enjoy I her company. So far, we've had a few coffee dates, so I know we can relax in each other's company, which is important. We were introduced to each other as two people who were both looking for marriage, and we got on well with each other, which was clear from our texts. Yes, the friendship is growing, but right now, I don't know if love can grow. At the moment, it's at the level of deepening regard and growing affection. She seems like a good woman, and I hope that if things keep developing, she might be my wife someday. If I didn't think that we could be successful, I wouldn't be driving so late at night to get to her.

Culturally, there is a method to getting married that is in line with my principles. It starts with being friends, then her being my girlfriend, then fiancée, and then, finally, wife. We can't skip any stage because each stage reveals a lot about someone's character. Right now, we are between friends and her being my girlfriend. If I could find it in my heart to really love her and that feeling were mutual, we could move forward. Girlfriend stage is the point at which she would be introduced to my family properly, and everything would start getting official. I definitely did not want to share anything until I know that she is 'the one' because I don't want Mum and my aunties to start getting overexcited thinking that there is a wedding on the horizon.

The thing I need to know—and when I say know, I mean, I really need to know in my heart of hearts—is if we are a fit.

Until then, my job is to protect this budding relationship to see if it flowers. Some brothers from the mosque suggested praying *Isthikhara* (the guidance prayer) although I want to wait until I know her better, and I'm sure the chemistry won't fizzle out.

The voice is onto something: a nagging feeling grows inside me because I know the questions don't stop here. I had practiced the justification before, so I temper it with a reasonable tone.

The voice points out, "If you are being reasonable, why do you feel guilty?" The conflict comes from the fact that I had prayed the *Juma prayer* (Friday prayer) with the brothers at lunchtime and the *Maghreb* (evening prayer) before I left home, but here I am a few hours later rushing to see her when I should be praying *Isha* (night prayer). There is a conflict in me, and the voice knows it.

Mona has a sort of vulnerability that appeals to me, and I want to look after her even though I know she is an accomplished and independent woman. She has an important job working in finance in the city. Mona lives alone, and that is the root of the uncomfortable feeling. Spending time alone with Mona wasn't a bad thing in our dating situation, but it just wasn't ideal.

The voice chimes in knowingly, "But at this time of night, going to see her could lead to sex." I recognize this as a very real risk. We have been meeting in public, and this is the first time she has asked me to come back to her place. I absolutely do not have plans to have sex with her tonight or even before we are married, but at the same time, I don't want to disappoint her. Is she expecting sex tonight? A big part of me does not want to sin intentionally with her and then sit on my prayer mat to ask forgiveness for my premeditated sin.

"Is she going to test my faith tonight?" the omnipotent voice asks.

"Maybe," I think. Sex always creates complexity, and I don't want to take our relationship there when at this stage, sex could easily tip the delicate balance of our introduction. I want to step with caution.

My doubt is not that Mona and I are mismatched. My problem is that she doesn't seem to be a practicing Muslim as I am.

Initially, when I started looking for marriage, I looked for women who labeled themselves as religious, but I found that it's a problem to classify someone this way. Sometimes, I did not seem religious enough to the women I met, or I did not have a big, long beard to convince the religious, hijab-wearing Muslim women that I was sincere in my faith. With Mona, I am the more religious one.

My reasonable response to the voice is, "It is normal to have a girlfriend, for at least a little while in this modern society. That is what all my friends do. I shouldn't feel guilty; after all, my intention is pure, right?" This is the only retort I can muster. The voice, set on tormenting me, is silent.

Feeling victorious, I rev the bike. This empowers me. My bike and body as one, I continue to divide wind and rain and push myself onward.

The voice interrupts my newfound celebration of freedom, "Tell her you pray. Tell her you're religious. Tell her the truth."

Instinctively, I say to myself, "No! She might run!"

She's probably not into religious men, and I'll be in the friend zone forever. I have been paying attention, and she hasn't uttered a single *InshAllah* (all hope is with God) or *MashAllah* (praise be to God) commonly uttered phrases amongst God-conscious Muslims. I hope that her reluctance with these phrases is because of her corporate training, which has maybe masked her instinct to praise her creator in public.

I can't ignore the words uttered by the voice. They rob me of my empowerment, and as a consequence, my inner peace.

The voice, brutal as always, goes in for the kill. "You know she's not the one for you, and you'll go there and sin, just like you're planning."

My reaction to this ugly truth is anger. "God damn you, voice! You always know how to mess things up."

I have been trying to avoid thinking about my need for sex and the growing feeling of lust that I feel when I am with her. I am struggling to keep things on a spiritual justification level. Like a haggard, bitter woman living in my head, the voice speaks its ugly truth.

That voice has been there all my life. Some people call it consciousness or anxiety. I call it a pain in the ass. On bad nights, it can keep me from sleeping by putting ideas into my head, giving me anxiety about the future, and providing over-analysis of the past. It keeps my mind whirring, its only purpose to rob me of peace of mind. It creates exhaustion and depression. Thoughts, thoughts, and more thoughts in an endless cycle. Sometimes, I just can't shut it up. It confuses me to the point where I can't function. My mind is as busy as rush hour. The voice is debilitating.

The voice commands, "Turn around, don't go! Tell her you practice your faith, and that you're not comfortable meeting her in private like this. Otherwise, you're getting to know her while hiding who you really are and that is not fair."

I know that the voice is right.

I can't bear the brutal truth. My response is rebellion, so I fix my course to Mona's house. I grip the handlebars tighter and rev the bike, going faster and faster while I slice the water on the slick roads with my front tire. My inner debate has distracted me from the quiet roads, and I don't notice my illegal speeds.

I also haven't noticed the little red car ahead of me. It rolls into the junction nearly fifteen yards in front of me from the adjoining side road on the left. As if in slow motion, it creeps quietly into the middle of the road like a stealthy lioness hunting in the Masai Mara.

The reality is that I am driving too fast, and I'm too close to swerve. As I move closer, the little car seems like an impenetrable tank, its red draining into the gray surroundings. It forms a barrier in my path, put there purposefully to stop me. I only notice it when it is in the middle of the road and it suddenly turns on its headlights, opening its eyes as if to say, "Abdul! I'm here, and you cannot escape."

Instinctively, I hit my brakes. The shrill sound of my tires on the wet road creates a sound that vibrates and echoes in the night. Other cars, trees, and the asphalt all act to amplify the sound. The deathly screech of my brakes penetrates my helmet, and it is the only thing I hear. This is the initial sensation before the impending impact of my bike and this car. This is the sound of horror. This is the finality of death.

I'm an experienced driver, and I know better. Usually, I don't drive this fast, and I would have just stopped and sworn angrily at this Sunday driver who forgot to turn on their lights. Today, there is no stopping. We are too close to each other, which limits my options. I calculate that even if I can swerve to the front or the back of the car, each action will still result in a devastating crash, with the slimmest chances of minimizing damage.

My single headlight reveals a flash of long blonde hair in the driver's seat, showing me that my irresponsible speeding is not just about my life—tonight, I have made decisions that will affect her too. I pray that, whoever she is, I haven't stolen her life.

I swerve toward the front, and I close my eyes tightly as I prepare for impact.

For a millisecond, the screeching of tires continues as my front wheel meets her front wheel. Her right front tire immediately explodes from the force of the impact. My bike, unstoppable, continues to try to drive over the hood of her car as if it is some insignificant barrier. Another millisecond later and my front tire explodes, exposing the rim, which travels forward like an inelegant circular saw, shredding the previously unscathed hood and hacking at the engine underneath it. Holes in the hood spew steam, sparks, and smoke.

The front of my bike comes to a stop as it chews the metal of her hood, and it firmly plants itself into the engine of her car. The violence of our mangled, metal vehicles looks like a vulgar modern art exhibit. The front motion of my bike stops, but my back wheel continues, acting as a springboard to launch my body into the unrestricted air space above the crash. I am flying.

There is beauty in knowing that you are living your last moments. The terror of the screeching subsides as I am thrown above the car and suspended in the air. As I accept the inevitability of my death, I reach a moment of inner calm, feeling serene as a result of my surrender. I am not in control of my life; I doubt I ever was.

So concentrated is the feeling of peace that it drowns out all sound—I hear nothing. Peace removes me from my body and makes me a spectator at my own death. My body takes the form of a black, leather star. My legs are above my head, and my arms are outstretched. I dare to open my eyes. I see Sophie—somehow, my soul knows her name—the owner of the blonde hair in the driver's seat of the red car. I see her face properly for the first time as I fly upside down.

Through the visor of my helmet, my eyes find hers. With a sense of purpose, I look at her to try to say, "I want forgiveness for robbing you of your life." We look directly at each other. She looks like a beautiful tragedy, her pale, oval face accented by her straight, blonde hair and bright blue, horror-stricken eyes. Mouth wide open, she is paralyzed, unable to produce a scream. I guess she is in her mid-thirties, but the fear on her face robs her of any other emotion. She wears a wedding ring on her left hand, and this gives me comfort. If she gets through this, someone will look after her. Her white knuckles show the vice-like grip she has on the steering wheel, and tear tracks, accentuated by mascara, run down her cheeks.

Our eyes are locked in this moment of human connection, this horror that neither of us wants to experience alone. It feels like a millennium as we stare at each other; we are one as the horror and violence erupts.

The glass of the windshield shatters around us. Glass indiscriminately cuts into Sophie's face, and some of it travels upward, penetrating my leathers and smashing into the visor of my helmet. Shards of glass cut into my body and hers.

Jenny, a beautiful little girl, is launched from the backseat of the car. I hadn't even seen her before.

The terror on Sophie's face multiplies. A mass of curly, blonde hair with a red tartan coat follows the shattered glass and flies like a missile from the backseat. I do not see her face, but I am aware of her. Her small body flies beneath mine, and she travels at a speed far faster than mine. My arms are outstretched toward her, trying desperately to catch her. Jenny is like a rugby ball, and I am an inept player who knows he will miss the catch.

The voice says, "She will die first." I know this is true. I also know that it was never my destiny to save her.

Shards of glass look like diamonds in her hair as they reflect the ghostly orange of the streetlamps. As Jenny travels through the windshield, the remaining glass snatches at her body and her clothes, as if trying to stop her.

She hits the ground on the front of her delicate little body with a violent thud. She skids three feet on the asphalt, each inch of road claiming a few grams of flesh, blood, and once-perfect golden locks of hair. Once the clothes settle on her fragile body, only her curls reflect the velocity and distance she travelled. Glass glints in between her locks, and her hair looks like it is filled with diamonds. The spreading blood starts to matte her hair.

Jenny isn't moving, and I am to blame. I killed her. My arms extend toward her, but I land on the asphalt road, first my arm, shattering into a million pieces, and then my torso hits with a hard thud that immediately breaks several of my ribs, piercing my heart and lungs. Finally, my neck smashes against the cold, wet road and the inside of my helmet. My windpipe is instantly ruptured by the broken pieces of bone from my spine. The crunching noise of my bones rings loudly in my ear. It is the last sound I hear.

As I lie in the road, the only warmth I feel is the blood escaping my body. It warms my skin, a damp, metallic warmth reminiscent of the fluid in the amniotic sack of my mother's womb. The agony makes it impossible to scream. I prepare to die, and my body begins the physical process of shutting down. My eyes are transfixed on the blurred bundle of Jenny. The excruciating pain fades into numbness. The numbness spreads, masking every sensation in my body.

The voice screams, "Wait! This is it!"

In my heart, I murmur *La-illah-il-Allah'* (There is no God but God). This is the creed of a Muslim, the statement that negates all of existence only to affirm the existence of the Creator.

My heart has made this final declaration, as strong as a heartbeat. My mouth does not produce the words; it can only muster blood bubbles accompanied by gurgles. There is no distinction to the human ear between my last declaration and the rattled breath that escapes me. With all my consciousness, I picture my index finger on my right hand in the pointing motion made while praying as I declare my faith, my imperfect faith.

The knowledge that I am responsible for the death of a little girl and possibly her mother with my careless driving makes me sad. Maybe I don't deserve good in my human life, but I still hope for a good death. Is this selfish? With a brief glimmer of hope, I start to become aware of my surroundings as they change, and the earthly dimension takes on a wider view and new spectrum.

I can see his shoes as he crouches beside me, listening to my heart and the whispered bubbles of blood that escaped my opened mouth in my last declaration of faith. He is with me, and I am not alone. He leans forward and touches my exposed, broken shoulder. His touch is cold, unfeeling, and final.

With his touch, my last breath and heartbeat come to a final stop. Life escapes the prison of my body. Numbness envelops me as my soul is taken out of my mouth in a final exhale. My eyes follow my soul, and it all seems vaguely familiar, like a suppressed memory of my soul entering my body while I was being formed in my mother's womb.

The separation is complete. My soul and my body are separate entities.

My soul stands beside him. I stand beside Azrael. I knew this day would come. Together, we stare at my broken body. Blood and flesh cover the asphalt road.

He lets me stare at my body, the frail vessel that I am emotionally attached to. He says nothing, even though I feel there is a lot to ask and to say. Time does not exist in my new dimension. I can only tell you it felt like I stood there for a few minutes before I turned to look at him and acknowledge that he was standing next to me.

There was no black cape or sickle in sight. Azrael is a genuinely handsome man, which is strange because archangels aren't described as being handsome. He stands expressionless and authoritative, and I know I trust him. Upon seeing his face and feeling his presence, I am calm. He heard my last proclamation of faith, and it is his job to remove my soul from my body.

We look at each other, and after a few moments, he asks me if I am okay. He asks this without using his mouth—I can hear his words in my head. I say, "Yes." I am dead, but I am okay. Is that a strange thing to say?

He knows I am asking myself questions. He looks at me as if he has heard them many times before and explains, "Death is the opposite of birth. It is a change of state." He adds, "Many humans do not appreciate that life is a luxury."

Moments later, my sense of attachment to my body dissipates like cigarette smoke in the wind. My body, like my motorbike, is something that got me from Point A to Point B. It was a way I recognized and labeled myself, but it wasn't real. I step away from the pooled blood as these new thoughts about my body create an awareness I had never considered in my earthly form.

He looks at me and asks, "Do you know what comes next?"

I nod.

He turns toward Jenny's body, which still lies on the asphalt. Her body radiates light and love and is the brightest spirit of the night. He walks over to her, and I watch him work. Instead of the handsome man, the form in which he greeted me, he is a young lady with a kind face, trusting eyes, and a big smile.

1.2 JENNY

I am lying on the road. It's cold and wet. How did I get here? I'd been dreaming of the bedtime story Grandad Jack read to me. It had rabbits and rainbows and flowers and butterflies, which are my favorite things in the world. In my dream, I was riding a flying unicorn, like the ones I have in my secret pretend world. I was telling Grandad Jack about my secret world, and we had been talking about which flowers to grow in the princess's garden. Grandad Jack knows an awful lot about gardens, and he has the most beautiful flowers in his garden.

The floor is cold, my clothes are wet, and my tummy hurts. I think I'm alone. Where is Mummy? I'm about to start calling for her when I see the other lady. She isn't Mummy, but she looks like someone I know. I feel like I've met her before. Maybe she's an aunty, one of Mummy's friends. It doesn't matter who she is because I feel like she's my friend. She leans over where I lie on the floor. She looks kind, and I like her right away. She pulls out a lollipop from her pocket. I'm a big girl, so I don't need a lollipop. I smile at her, and she smiles back at me. She touches me on my forehead, and her hand is warm like when Mummy holds me still to braid my hair. My toes tingle like someone is trying to tickle me, but then I start to feel cold. The cold feeling spreads so fast that I can't feel my body, and my throat makes a funny noise. I close my eyes.

When I open them, I am standing next to the lady and holding her hand. She is on her knees, so we are looking at each other eye to eye. She offers me the lollipop again, so I take it and put it in my mouth. Mummy told me not to go with strangers, but this nice lady doesn't feel strange. I ask her, "Have you seen my Mummy?"

She doesn't answer that question. Instead, she asks me how I am. With the lollipop in my mouth, I tell her I am fine. She asks me if I know what's happening. I think about that.

I nod at her. It was in my dream.

I am wearing my favorite princess dress, and my hair is in ponytails. I have my lollipop in my hand, and I feel very happy.

She asks me, "Do you know where we are going?" I tell her that I want to be in Heaven with Granny, Grandpa, and my cat, Fluffy. She smiles at me.

I was dreaming about unicorns when some angels interrupted it. They told me that I had to leave this Earth and that I was going to die. They said they would put me in a very deep sleep I wouldn't wake up from, but that's ok because I am going to be with Fluffy, Granny, and Grandpa. They told me that I shouldn't worry.

She smiles at me again. She says to me, "Before we can go, darling, you need to do something for your Mummy if you want to help her."

I can't believe how quickly I forgot about Mummy! I don't know where she is, and that makes me a little bit upset, like the time I didn't listen to her and got lost in the supermarket. I got so upset that day, and Mummy was upset, too.

I trust this lady. She tells me that Mummy is here and that Mummy is sleeping right now. Even though she is sleeping, Mummy can still hear me. She tells me that Mummy will be a little bit upset when she wakes up and that I can help Mummy to be not too upset. I love helping Mummy. I used to help her in the kitchen. Mummy calls me her little helper.

The nice lady tells me that with every little piece of strength I have, I should tell Mummy that I love and forgive her, but only if that is true in my heart.

Well, that's not hard because of course it's true. I shout out, "Mummy, I love you."

I think that maybe I won't see Mummy for a little while, and this makes me sad. I don't want to be away from her.

The nice lady hears my thoughts and says, "Don't worry! Mummy and you will be together one day." She reminds me that I need to help Mummy right now.

I stand in my dress with the nice lady, and I hold her warm hands. Closing my eyes, I see my Mummy's beautiful face.

I say, "I love you, Mummy, and don't worry about me. I'm going to be with Granny, Grandpa, and Fluffy."

I have a vision of my Mummy's face, and she looks upset. I quickly add, "Oh, and Mummy, I love you and forgive you."

I can see tears on Mummy's face, same like she gets after she's been speaking with Daddy sometimes. She is crying, but she is smiling too. I know Mummy and Daddy don't want me to go, and that they love me very much, but God wants me to come to Him, and this is what is meant to be. I hope that they will be happy again, like in their old photos from before I was born. I will be waiting for them, but I have to wait on the other side. They don't have to worry—I won't be alone.

After that, I feel happy. I don't like to see Mummy upset, but I know she was smiling behind her tears. Maybe Daddy can kiss away Mummy's tears, just like Mummy kisses away mine. The nice lady tells me I did a great job and that we need to go.

As the lady stands up, a bright white light appears in the middle of the street. We walk toward the white light. As we get closer, I see it is a tunnel of light from the sky. At the bottom of the tunnel are huge feathers that belong to a powerful winged angel standing inside the light.

His feathers open, and inside them he holds Granny, Grandpa, and Fluffy. Grandpa is holding Fluffy. They have come to get me, and I am very happy to see them. The angel who brought them has huge feathers, bigger than I have ever seen. He must be very strong to hold all my family. He looks friendly too, as he has a big smile for me. The man nods at the nice lady to say hello.

Granny and Grandpa rush forward to hug me. We hold each other tightly, and we kiss each other. They pull me into the circle of the angel's arms, and Fluffy jumps from Grandpa's arms into mine. As I stroke him, I feel whole, warm, loved, and I feel like I am home.

They tell me they have been waiting for me and that they want to introduce to me other people from our family. I love them so much, and I missed them all the time they were gone. The nice lady steps back, and I am in Grannie's arms, petting Fluffy and sucking my lollipop when I see him.

I forgot about him since I met this nice lady, but that is Abdul. He died with me tonight. I don't know how I know his name, but I know we met tonight. I know that he is a nice man, even though he killed me. He looks at me, his eyes asking me to forgive him, but there isn't anything to forgive. This accident was meant to happen, and we always would have met like this. I smile at him, so that he knows we are ok, and he smiles back.

As Grannie, Grandpa, and I cuddle in the light, the angel's feathers close around us, and that's when I leave Earth.

1.3 SOPHIE

I am in a blissful state, I am aware of nothing around me. I only remembered that the office Christmas party was tonight, and I had been looking forward to it for weeks. I planned to have a few drinks, so I left Jenny with her Grandad Jack. Jenny loved Grandad Jack. They would talk for hours and tell each other stories. They always looked for opportunities to spend time together. Jack lived near the tube station, so it was easy to get to his house. I had arranged to pick up Jenny the next day on my supermarket run, so I left my car at Jack's house, as I had planned to catch a cab home.

Tonight, I couldn't wait a single moment longer to be with her. What had been the rush to bring her home? I can't remember.

The memory of my boss kissing me seeped into my mind. That was it. I wanted to bring Jenny home so that I could remind myself that my family was important. Having Jenny at home with me and my husband Craig, who I had been with for over fifteen years, would drive away the demons of the Christmas party infidelity.

My boss, Daniel, was a nice guy, and we harmlessly flirted all the time even though he knew I was married. I could have shot down his advances and put him in his place, but I liked the attention. My husband Craig hasn't given me attention for such a long time that I didn't even look for it from him anymore. Our marriage wasn't bad, but it wasn't what it used to be. The passion had passed for the predictably mundane. I often questioned myself: did I have unrealistic expectations of our marriage now that we had been together for fifteen years? None of my answers changed the fact that I feel like Craig doesn't value me and doesn't show me love. He tolerated me; in fact, we tolerated each other. Years of responsibilities and paying mortgages and bills had taken their toll on our marriage. We have drifted apart and become different people with different interests, paddling hard to stay above water and protect our perfect life. Years have passed, and that reality has made itself at home in our marriage. I have slowly grown accustomed to drinking my way to the bottom of a bottle (or two) of wine most nights, while he sits at his computer. The frustration of our marriage is a joke to me. We live together, but we have separate lives.

The Christmas party had ended in the pub. Daniel wanted me to come back to his house, so when he went to the toilet, I escaped to get back to my family. I had never physically cheated on Craig before and although our marriage was loveless, I knew cheating on Craig with Daniel would be an easy and convenient option—nothing more. It was that cold, calculated thought that allowed me to pull away from the party and get a head start toward the train home.

Drunken eyes showed me the young lovers in the corner, kissing so vigorously they were almost eating each other, and then suddenly stopping when they realized people were watching. I know I loved Craig like that once, with the purest passion. Craig was my rock when my parents died. He had carried me through the darkest times in my life. I hate to think of those days, not because of the loss I experienced, but because I was a shell of the woman I am now. I was a quivering wreck, unable to process the deaths of my parents, who died weeks apart. My vulnerability had made me feel so weak, and it was then that I decided that my weakness was grotesque. I had become so undesirable that I made a decision to strengthen myself from my core. As an extreme reaction to that weakness, I chose to become fiercely independent. This bravado impacted my marriage, but I emerged like a phoenix from the ashes and reinvented myself as bulletproof. As time progressed, I saw less and less value in Craig. In fact, he reminded me of the sniveling schoolgirl I was reduced to in my darkest hour. I looked at myself for the first time in a long time, and I wanted to feel that sense of passion again for the man I had once loved. I wanted to come home and sit on our sofa with old photos in my hands, our daughter on my lap and my husband next to me as we recounted our adventures and planned new ones —something we hadn't done in a long time. Just for one second, I wanted to reconnect with Craig to see if we could still share the same dreams.

It made me tearful that my life was like this. The tears were honest, and they fell in big, wet burning droplets from my eyes. They were real, and they represented years of my frustrations and bitterness. The cold person I had become was my biggest reason to cry. I had calculated the lack of value I saw in Craig against the opportunity that Daniel represented. I was stupid enough to risk everything I had worked for a fleeting feeling. I could have done what I wanted with Daniel. The act of infidelity didn't scare me, but the irrelevance of my marriage was damning. The statistic my marriage would become and the personality I had developed scared me. I didn't recognize myself anymore. Jenny, my daughter, was the best result of my marriage, and I wanted her with me now. When my station came, I exited the train and fumbled in my handbag for my tube ticket, and somehow my car keys found their way into my hand.

It was a short walk to Jack's house from the station. The clean air helped clear my head. I chewed gum to freshen my breath and removed the smeared makeup before I knocked on his door. My frosty relationship with Craig had found its way into my relationship with his dad, Jack, which was convenient because I didn't need to hug or kiss him. He was no longer used to personal familiarity with me, so he couldn't smell the alcohol oozing from the pores of my skin.

A brief exchange later and he handed me Jenny, who was asleep. I managed to bundle her into the backseat of the car. I didn't bother with the car seat because the straps were too hard to figure out in the dark, and if I had taken ages to do them, Jack would have come over to help.

Before the drinking and driving laws were so strict, I had driven loads of times when I was tipsy. I knew that if I went slowly nothing would happen. I carefully drove out of Jack's driveway and along his road toward the junction. The roads were clear, but when I got to the middle of the junction, I realized my headlights were off. I reached down and turned them on.

After that, I am aware of nothing, which is a blissful state to be in until I start to feel a horrible pain that seeps into my consciousness. Pain comes in waves. It takes over my body, and a sixth sense tells me that something very bad has happened. With the pain is a panic that starts to bubble inside me. It begins in the pit of my stomach, a persistent burning rising inside me. I am slow to realize that I cannot feel the presence of Jenny. I feel that she is not with me, and that scares me most of all. My distress is rooted in her missing energy. As a mother, my gut instinct tells me that a valuable light has gone out. I can't sense her, and I know that my heart is connected to my little girl, so my mother's instinct is asking, "Where is Jen? Where is my little girl?"

These thoughts subtly let me know that she is not with me. She isn't here.

My heart reminds me of a very recent memory in which I heard her say she loves me and forgives me, an experience of pure serenity and beauty. In my heart, I also know it is a goodbye, and that thought is in the process of smashing my heart with a sledgehammer. My body reacts to what I recognize as the truth, and I can't breathe, my chest can't expand. All of my air has been expelled, and this intensifies the burning in my stomach. Worse than my broken body and soul is my breaking heart, which heard my six-year-old daughter say goodbye.

What has happened? Is my body broken? Am I paralyzed? I can't move; I can't breathe. I know my car is broken. My life is broken. My sense of loss is strangling me. A dark shadow towers over me. The sun will never shine again.

As consciousness starts to reform in my mind, I instinctively start pleading to God, "Don't take my little Jenny, God! Anything but that! Please don't take her away from me!"

If I could sob and wail, I would, but I can't move. I don't know what's going on. If I were conscious, I would scream at the top of my lungs. What is this: Distress? Panic? It is so much more than fear.

Cruel, guttural snarling startles me. It surrounds me as it gets louder and closer. The cold breath of a pack of wolves or some other unworldly beings is close to my face, breathing into my ear. They have come for me, and they want me, I know. They are here for me, and I deserve them. The evil beings that live in the shadows, that watch us in our daily lives, are awaiting permission to torment me. Their vile breath makes my spine shudder. We can sense these creatures in our world, if only for a fleeting moment, but it's only when we are in a different dimension that we genuinely feel their presence, their menace, their threat. They surround the smashed car, and I know they are here for me. I should be scared. I should be wetting myself, but only my daughter saying goodbye strikes genuine fear in my heart.

I can't feel her presence. I only sense them.

"God! Do what you want to me, but please don't take my Jenny," I pray for the first time.

A voice chimes in, distracting me from my prayer. "I am a rubbish human being and I do not deserve a blessing like Jenny. After all, I have not been a good wife." I can't turn back time. I know what I have done, and I am ready to take responsibility for it. That's why I need Jenny to be at home with me to remind me what is real.

I know I shouldn't be behind the steering wheel. I was stupid to risk driving drunk. Typically, it's a journey I can do with my eyes closed, driving from Jack's house to ours, but I forgot to turn on the headlights. When I did turn them on, that's when that motorcyclist came from nowhere, and that's when I killed him. The realization of what happened hits me hard, and I know now there will be a high price to pay.

I was negligent with my marriage, with the car seat, with the motorcyclist. I know this situation is crazy. My baby's loss is too high a price to pay for my stupidity.

The steely smell of the unworldly creatures fills my car. They are so close; they know they nearly have me. They can have me if I killed my little girl! I am not worthy of life or redemption.

"Oh, God! Please not my little girl. I love her, take me but not her." My love for Jenny overflows into ferocious, unrelenting prayer. "Let her live with her father and have a good life. Let her fall in love, let her get married, let her feel the joy of being a Mum." I pray hard. "She deserves a chance. I'm the sinner, God. Take me. I don't deserve life, God! Please, take me," I plead as desperation sinks in.

A voice in my head compassionately informs me, "She's gone. Jenny is gone, and tonight you killed a man." I feel the brutality of truth. Those words smash my ears like a ton of bricks. I repeat them in my head. There is no comfort or solace as they flood my mind with images that I don't want to see.

I've proclaimed my atheism for such a long time now that praying is a new experience. Right now, with my body unable to move, I am at the height of my vulnerability. The unworldly creatures crowd around my car and wait to dig their knife-like claws into my skin. I have no other hope now that my angel, Jenny, is gone, and I wait for an answer to my prayers.

"I recognize that I need you, God," I pray, knowing the voice in my head will say something to retort. I ignore it as I speak with God directly in my fragile, human state.

From my heart, I plead, "I'm a rubbish person, but right now I submit to you, and I come willingly. Please, make sure my little girl is safe and happy. If she isn't, please take me and return her to her Dad. Please give my husband Craig happiness. He is a good man, and he deserves a woman who appreciates him. A woman unlike me, a woman who won't get frustrated and spend a lifetime pushing him away and getting drunk. If you want to throw me to the pack of creatures, I'll go willingly to Hell. Please fix my mistakes, and create happiness for Jenny and Craig."

The last time I had such a frank conversation with God was when I decided to give up believing in Him; that was at the grand age of nine. I made it clear in our chat that I was going to stop knocking on his door because He was busy helping other people, and I didn't need His help. I had prided myself on my atheism. My parents hadn't approved of my decision, but they were the 'live and let live' sort, and they tried not to stuff religion down my throat. I think, secretly, they believed I would follow them to church one day.

Giving up on God in later years made great dinner party conversation. I learned that my atheism equated me with being smart, scientific, and independent. At the end of the day, no one can be more independent than someone who is independent of God.

But right now, forget independence and misplaced identity: I need God's help. God is all I have, so I pray. It is instinctual, it is natural, it is true, and it is all I can do.

My daughter is away from me. My mind doesn't want to acknowledge what my heart is telling me: that she had died tonight by my negligence and that I had murdered a motorcyclist in the process. This was the worst and possibly the last night of my life.

The growling grows closer, and multiple creatures inside and outside my car surround me until their metallic breath dampens my hair. The frost of their breath gives me icy chills. The intense pain in my stomach burns as if Hell is inside me. The cold and the heat make me physically want to submit to their wrath. The truth of my missing Jenny keeps me mentally kicking. I want to fight this situation with prayer. The unworldly creatures are so close, and my prayers have no answer. Has time run out? I can't give up and drift away. I need an answer.

In my desperation, the voice breaks into the silence. "Ask for one more chance, so you can fix things." Can I possibly ask God, who I have denied for most of my life, for something more? Can I ask God for another shot? Is that possible? My options aren't great, so I ask God for another chance, to try my hardest to make things better, and to try my best to live a life of hope.

Before I even comprehend the enormity of what I am asking, a meek voice springs from me. "Please, God, let me fix this." I whisper because I have no right to ask, no right to attempt a negotiation.

"Please God, I will be more grateful. I will be appreciative. I'll do my best to fall in love with you. I promise, I will find a path to you, God. I will find a way to love my husband again. I will honestly try to make my marriage work. I have already given up drinking." I knew this was true. I carry on, repeating these solemn vows. A sense of hope starts to grow, and with it a sense of purpose and a shimmer of strength. These promises provide a path back to humanity, back to life.

After a lifetime, the snarling subsides and the unworldly creatures inch back from my ear, my face, my body, and then my car, their hairy bodies paling into the shadows where they live. As I move back into the earthly dimension, my bodily pain becomes excruciating, each wave of pain getting worse and worse. If I were conscious, I would be screaming. This pain is worse than any I had ever known before. Slowly at first and then with growing speed, I can feel the adrenaline start to pump in my body. I return from a dimension where I was waiting for judgment, and I come back to life.

I can make out the faint blue lights as an ambulance arrives, and I hear sirens. This is my first indication that my prayer has been accepted. As I sit in the car, I drift in and out of dimensions. I see the motorcyclist, and I feel his presence. He is a young man standing next to his crumpled body on the road.

He looks at me and whispers, "Choose life. Choose God. Choose love. I forgive you."

I muster a vague smile in acknowledgement of his kind words. They are beautiful words of advice that I might not remember when I wake, but they will always leave a profound mark on my soul.

My heart knows I killed my daughter, and that knowledge is enough to drown me, but his forgiveness lightens my heavy heart. With the motorcyclist's words and Jenny's words, I know it was our destiny to meet, even if it isn't on an earthly plane.

Can I dare to have hope in my heart? God hasn't thrown me to the wolves. I must be worthy of redemption. With these painful thoughts, I take my first fateful step to recovery. Using all of my remaining strength, I try to open my eyes.

A nurse is here with an ambulance crew and the fire service. She stands next to a fireman using a huge saw to cut my broken body out of the car. The nurse sees the slight fluttering of my eyelids and signals the fireman to stop cutting the car door. She leans into my car, and her warm hand touches my throat. She screams, "We've got a pulse!"

1.4 AZRAEL

Tonight was an ordinary night with scenes I have seen many times before and will see many times again.

Jenny and Abdul, like all the souls before them, do not understand the length of time that passed since their souls and bodies parted. They cannot perceive the sheer number of eyes on them as they transitioned from their worldly realm into the afterlife.

Innocence always gets a heads start, and Jenny seamlessly transitioned into the Heavenly Kingdom.

Abdul didn't perceive that his righteous actions of prayer, charity, and his connection with his Qur'an had been walking alongside him. These actions stand beside him as an impenetrable bodyguard shielding him from the demons of hell.

Although they never met in their earthly lives, Abdul and Jenny's destinies were long intertwined.

Where there is repentance, there is benevolence. Sophie will make better choices, and loss will be her teacher and guide. I will come for her after twenty-four years, three months, and seven days, at a quarter past three.

It is my duty to fulfill the death commandments, and you in your human format cannot comprehend me. Understand that I am unlike anything you know; you cannot fathom the duty bestowed upon me. You live in a dimension with physical laws of time and space and the restrictions that those laws bring—these laws that have no impact on me. For those who think they can cheat death, they only cheat themselves. Simply put, if you were born, you will die.

I do not judge you. Judging you is not my task. I observe you until the command is given to collect your soul, so it is pointless to fear me. Fear, in reality, does not exist. It is just a construct of your frail mind.

If you are scared of the thought of our meeting, you should be. But know this: Humans never die alone. I am always present, and I will always be with you. You will always go where you are meant to be, even though the blessing of life means you exercise your free will for now.

Like everyone before you and after you, our appointment time is written. My parting advice is that if you are inclined to prepare for our meeting, cement your faith with good deeds. Your death is the only thing you can count on in life.

When your time comes, I will find you.

King Solomon & the Cat

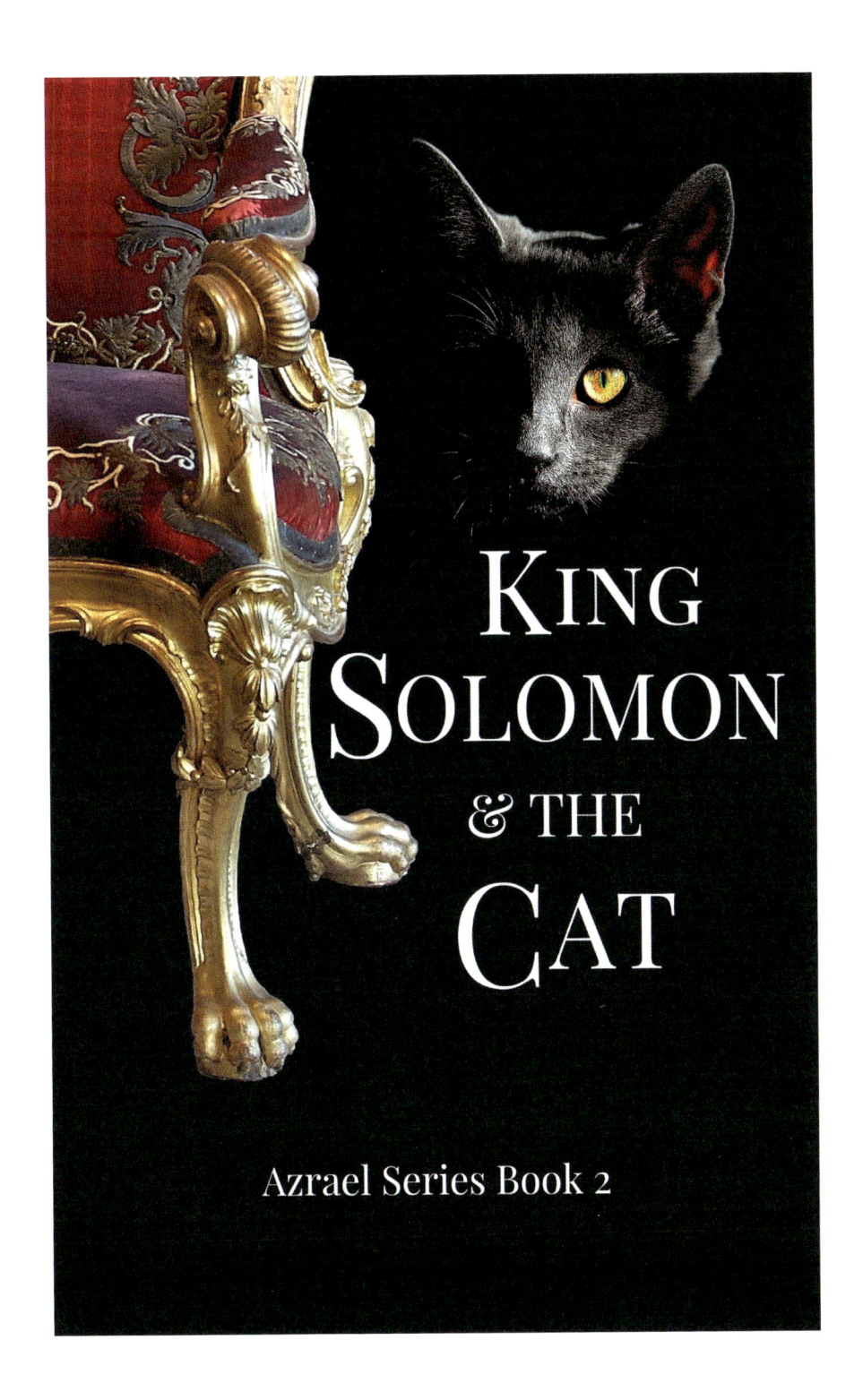

Azrael Series Book 2

2.1 PROTECTING GRAVES

The young cat had an audience. How unfortunate; it hadn't anticipated this. The young cat hadn't realized that its first kill was a rite of passage, and the elders within the cat community would come to watch him handle his prey. He didn't understand that he should handle his prey with prowess and pride. The elders would rely on him to feed them in their old age, so they had a vested interest in his hunting skills, but he was too young to realize the implications of the audience. He was also too young to understand that holding a pigeon by its wing as it flapped the other freely was not correct. Incompetence was all that the elders saw.

The cat, too young to comprehend the politics of the situation, held his trophy with pride. The elders watched with displeasure as they realized there was much to teach this little cat, and until it learned, there would be lean times ahead for all of them. This would make life difficult for the little cat and his family, who would be ostracized from the community.

The cat trainer had exposed the young cat, and he should never have let the elders see this poor display. He should have trained the young cat to a higher standard before parading his first kill, which was anything but dead.

My displeasure wasn't with the young cat, as I didn't believe it was his fault. It was very much the fault of his trainer, who should have known better—and, in fact, did know better. The trainer and I glared at each other. I scowled at him to show that I knew he had purposefully outed the young cat. It was no secret in the cat community that the trainer had a young cat of his own, so it was evident that the trainer hoped his son would one day lead the hunt for the cats of the graveyard and hold the social standing the title brought. Unfortunately for the trainer, I knew his motive, and sabotage was a dirty game. I glared at him, and he reciprocated. Our bodies were rock solid and set for the fight. He flexed his muscles at me to demonstrate his strength. I knew he would try, and I also knew I could bury this cat in an instant. He knew it, too. It wasn't just my superior strength or the fact that I stood on the side of right and truth. I was an unknown quantity to him. After all, I wasn't a cat—I was a shapeshifter. I could take the form of a person, an animal, or an animate object. Some cultures called me genie, and some called me jinn. I could bury him, and he knew it because I was nothing like him. My strength was beyond his comprehension, beyond any frame of reference that existed in his little cat brain. He knew he shouldn't mess with me, but tension built as we gave each other the evil eye.

A human man and woman walked past the graveyard and caught our interaction. They seemed to understand the situation and see the young cat with its mouthful of pigeon wing. God had sent the couple to see what was happening in the graveyard. They were more gifted than average humans, who did not understand what was going on around them. On seeing the young cat, the couple prayed for mercy for the pigeon.

God responded to their prayer and gave the young cat the intelligence to clasp the damaged pigeon with his paws and adjust his position. He held the pigeon with his jaws at the base of its neck, and a sigh of relief sounded all around as the bird slowly lost its life. The cat elders relaxed, and hope was restored. The humans' prayers were answered. My anger with the trainer had not subsided, but God had chosen to resolve the situation by sending the humans to visit instead of letting me brawl.

The pigeons' beating heart stopped, the damaged wing stilled, and finally, the pigeon died. The young cat had corrected himself and was officially a hunter. He ran off to show his mother his kill. It was a proud day for him: the pigeon was more than a third of his size, so it was a noteworthy achievement.

My interest was to see off the humans. They had seen enough of our community already. I came and stood outside the graveyard, hissing at them on the street. The human female approached me foolishly, but my crouched stance made her check herself. In my cat form, I was a graveyard cat, which meant I was certainly not for petting. I was a warrior and nothing like the docile, fat housecats she knew. Also, I had a job to do. The couple understood that they should leave the graveyard, and they walked away with only a brief hesitation. I returned to the cemetery to disband the elders.

My job was to protect the graves of the Jerusalem nobles buried in the graveyard. Humans saw me as a cat, but the people of the grave saw me as a fierce lion. The people of the graves were very perceptive: they knew it was my job to protect them. I am good at my job because I have been doing it for many years. I am an old soul, and I have seen much of life.

As a jinni, I am made of smokeless fire, and I can shapeshift into any living form. I can be another person—maybe someone you know—or an animal. Sometimes, you might only perceive my shadow, but most likely, you won't see me at all. There are malevolent jinn, and you might have heard stories about them. More commonly, there are Jinn like me. I have a job to do, and I am devoted to my job. Pious and strong, I can help if I choose to, and I can bring terror. The trainer cat backed down because he knew he was powerless against me, and fighting me would have led to his destruction.

You might wonder what the people of the grave need to be protected from.

My job in the graveyard was to protect the graves from negative energies, which sometimes came to disturb the peace. I simply worked with the regular cats to teach them to chase those negative energies away, which is why you always see cats in graveyards. I was sent to protect the people of the graves and to train these cats.

Recently, the attacks had lessened because that people in the cemetery were very strong in their faith. When they met their graves, their piety gave them abundant mercy. Over time, that mercy had spilled onto their immediate neighbours and then throughout the whole graveyard. Little by little, all the people of the grave were being affected by their pious neighbours. It was a domino effect starting from the godly souls recently buried in the graveyard.

I expected to be reassigned shortly. The regular cats had learned how to protect the people of the graves, and there was less for me to do; cat community politics and playing the chief of the place held no interest for me. Position and power were completely unattractive to me, as I considered myself a humble servant of God.

The reason for the increase in pious souls interested me, and I thought about following the trail. Where had these people come from?

I heard things, whispers from the humans and the jinn, about a new king. The day the graveyard job was done, I made a promise to myself to go see this new King. What was extraordinary about him? For the first time in many years, people being buried had light and mercy to accompany them.

All the community had been benefiting from the humans and jinn who walked around in the remembrance of their Lord. They were alive in their hearts, and it was a beautiful sight to behold. I even saw some of the malevolent jinn community soften and become pious. That fact was enough to tell me there was something remarkable about this king, and akin to the cat I pretended to be, I was curious.

I was resolute. As I slept, I had a dream. Dreams were the method through which I received my orders and understood where God wanted me to go. The message was unclear, although I knew that the time had come to move on.

The next day, I requested an audience with the eldest of the graveyard cat community. He was an old and wise cat. Many cats mistook his age for frailty, negating the years of life experience he had. They didn't understand that his age was his strength. He knew cats: their natures and psychologies. He was a cat that commanded respect. He had fought many battles in his time. Being a leader meant that he had fought physical and internal battles. Leader was a title of respect, given based on merit and no other measure. I told the old cat the time had come for me to leave, and that I entrusted the smooth running of the graveyard to him. He accepted my resignation and understood that the responsibility was now solely his. He knew his cats had been trained, and they would carry out the somewhat easier job of protection since the graveyard was so newly pious. I thanked him for welcoming me into his community, which was a formality, as there had been no welcome—just assimilation. He breathed a sigh of relief that I was leaving. My presence among the cats was controversial. They knew I was a more powerful being, and many of them felt unsettled; the unknown always unsettles. I respectfully said my goodbyes and left the community, having served there for many years. I left knowing its future was balanced. I would not look back.

I exited the graveyard for the last time and came into the domain of the living humans. They were a truly different sort of creation, and very unlike the people of the graves, who were either filled with sorrow or excitement at the prospect of the end of time and the promise of Heaven. The living humans were more like our jinn community than they realized. They carried on with their lives in meaningless pursuits. I didn't want their attention, so I kept myself in cat form and skulked around the sides of the roads to get to the market square, which backed the royal compound and made it a great point of entry to the Royal Palace.

It was not a coincidence that my orders came the night after I made my intentions clear, as I had seen many times that God had a plan.

The humans in the market haggled for the price of carrots, pomegranates, and sweets. Mankind was a fantastic creation, and so very self-absorbed. Life had been serving them for centuries, and they understood little about life. The market was different in that those people shopping still had an air of calm and a remembrance of God on their lips —and presumably in their hearts as well. It was a very different experience than when I had visited years ago and the merchants were stealing from the buyers with high prices and rigging scales that they used to measure wares. The interactions now between buyers and sellers were honest and humbling. Had I been in the graveyard so long? Why hadn't I noticed the change of mood in Jerusalem? Was this the impact of the new king? His presence was all that had changed in recent times, and all these signs increased my curiosity even more.

The plan was simple: to break into the palace and observe. I could take the form of a fly and sit on the wall to watch the comings and goings. I knew that if I observed for long enough, the truth would unfold. As jinn, we understood this from an early age. It is habit to keep to the shadows and watch mankind.

Stealthily, I crossed the market square and climbed a tree that would give me access to the royal compound. I climbed the tree with ease and jumped over the palace wall, landing in a flowerbed. While I sat among the flowers and shrubs, it occurred to me that I was visiting the king: I should attempt to clean my head and paws in case I was seen. I didn't want the humiliation of being chased out the palace, and I didn't want to take an invisible form because I had heard the jinn talking about the new king too, so I guessed that some had visited the palace. My firm faith often repelled other jinn, so I did not want attention from any of them. I licked my paws and cleaned my ears. It took quite a long time to bring myself above the graveyard standards for grooming.

I left the shrubs and walked into one of the many palace gardens. They were immaculate gardens with the greenest grass and most beautiful flowers, trees, and plants. Some were planted for decoration, some were clearly for healing purposes to prepare potions and tinctures, and some were for attracting wildlife. As I walked from one garden to another, I saw people in the distance sitting on the grass. Were they enjoying a picnic in the palace gardens? This was as good a place as any to begin my investigations. I walked forward silently and sat behind the people. The best thing about being a cat was that I didn't need to be close to hear everything, as my hearing was impeccable.

I made myself comfortable with a view of the humans' backs, and the human to my right turned to look at me. I didn't expect to be acknowledged. He nodded his head to greet me, and his eyes glinted a dull jade green that I understood. It was a signal only visible to me. He was a jinn in a human form. He had sensed that I was not just a cat. I was even more curious. Why was a jinni in plain sight of the humans in the palace gardens? I needed a better view of what was happening. I circled to the left, away from the jinni, so I could see and hear. I let the mortal men pet me and show me love. It was an emotion I was uncomfortable with, having lived so long in the graveyard. With each touch of my fur, I had to ensure I remained patient with the humans expressing their love for me. It was painful. My instinct was to scratch, but I accepted it as a test of my patience.

The men sat in a semicircle of fine silk rugs on the grass. Interspersed among them were tea glasses and fruit platters, and some of them wrote furiously while their leader spoke. They sat mesmerized, not wanting to miss a single word.

2.2 THE LESSON

The teacher of the study circle sat on a cushion placed on a fine silk rug. The rug was set on a plush green lawn. The only markers of his elevated status were his singular rug and cushion, and his position toward the front of the group.

He wore the best clothes and had the noblest face I had seen in all my many years of existence. He was a handsome young Arab man with thick, black hair and sun-kissed skin. His spoke with incredible knowledge. His words were wise, eloquent, and captivating. He spoke of the universe, the world, human nature, and the eternal struggle against the ego. He demonstrated a wisdom that was in conflict with his youthful appearance. His aura was white and peaceful, and submission to his Lord emanated from every pore.

As I relaxed into listening to this captivating man's speech and slowly let down my guard, he looked directly at me and called me to sit next to him. This in itself was not shocking, but the way he called shocked me to the core: he asked me to come sit with him in the way Jinn speak. I was astonished that a human had this capability.

It must be understood that the jinn can move and communicate so quickly that it is entirely unseen by humans. There were very few humans in history with the ability to speak directly to us. Typically, mankind and jinn don't interact; when a human wants to get ahead in life and tries to harness the power of the jinn, it never ends well. Here was a man who was extolling the beauty of God and able to speak with me so that none of the humans could tell. I had never come across anyone so gifted in all my existence. Furthermore, my cat appearance hadn't fooled him: he knew I was a jinni.

I moved warily forward. I had no intention of interacting with a human right now; I had only come to observe, and I felt unprepared for this meeting. The humans saw my wariness as I approached. Moving toward the teacher, the man these people had come to listen to, it was evident they revered and respected him. Some of the students had been so moved by their teacher that tears ran down their faces and they asked for mercy. They were unsure of my motives as I came close, so some of them tried to shoo me away. They hadn't heard the teacher call me, and they weren't aware of the fraction of a millisecond interaction between us.

One portly merchant raised his hand to try to shoo me away. He could see that I was a tatty graveyard cat sitting among the most influential men in the Jerusalem community, and I was approaching their teacher.

The teacher looked at the man and said, "Let him approach."

The protection was welcome from the merchant's raised hand, which had huge rings on his thick fingers. In my cat form, his rings would have seriously damaged me.

As I got closer, I started to understand what I was seeing. The teacher asked for a cushion. Patting the cushion, he motioned for me to sit next to him. I made my way onto the silk cushion filled with feathers, careful so that my claws didn't cut the silk. I tried to sit in one place, so my dirty fur wouldn't ruin too much of the fine materials. As I sat and attempted to relax, all eyes turned back to the teacher, and the lesson resumed.

My mistake was apparent as soon as the lesson began again; I had mistaken the teacher for a palace teacher—a domestic servant—when, in fact, this teacher was much more. This was King Solomon himself. It was obvious that King Solomon was an exceptional king. He could communicate with me, which made sense because I had heard the jinn speak about him with great affection. We jinn are rarely interested in the musings of human life, so I knew King Solomon was unique.

I noticed the birds in the trees perched and listening to the king. He had command of the animals, including insects, and a trail of ants sat off to one side to avoid being crushed underfoot. Later, I discovered he had command of the winds and could travel on them if he desired. He was an extraordinary man with many special and unusual gifts.

What I also learned about him that day was that I loved him from the deepest core of my heart. He was to me daylight reflecting the presence of the sun. His being a king was inconsequential. He was a prophet of God, and his powers were mirrored and praised God, and that made him my everything.

When I understood his prophetic presence and lineage, I knew that I would never leave this man. I would be in his service until my dying breath. I was grateful to be guided to him. He was a messenger of God living at the same time as me, and I was fortunate to be in his company. He had the deepest integrity, compassion, and humility. He was devoted and loving. It was evident that he was trusted, and his students were the elite of Jerusalem and Palestinian society, as well as me, a graveyard cat that trusted and respected him. We were his followers. We wanted his message of love, peace, and unity to emanate from us. His prophetic family lineage went back to the first man on earth, Adam, and he was a son of David. In his presence, we were connected to the voice of God. We heard the revelations of God through him. There was no option but to fall in love with this man.

The lesson was like nothing I had experienced before, the truth had no bounds, and King Solomon had no ego. His teachings were sent to mankind, the jinn, and the animals and insects, reflecting all our different worlds. Human beings could not distinguish when King Solomon was speaking with jinn and when he was speaking with the animals. Sitting beside him at the front of the class, I could see the sheer number of eyes on him.

Around him was absolute wealth: gold, silver, pearls, gemstones, and items made of intricate sandalwood and carvings that would have taken decades to complete. Everything was more beautiful than the eye could comprehend. Beauty was abundant in his palace and in the hearts of his subjects. Finally, the souls in the graveyard made sense. King Solomon was the wisest man I had ever met, and he spoke with purpose. He seemed to know me, to look through me, and to understand what measure of me was goodness and what needed work. Meeting him made me very conscious of my shortcomings in the eyes of my creator.

I stayed in the palace from this day onward and became a friend of King Solomon. We spoke about his decisions, and I learned from him. He liked me because of my unwavering devotion to duty and my God-conscious attitude. Finally, I had found a kindred spirit, a man whose value was his honorable heart.

What good fortune to be guided to this man. I was blessed. I often thought about this time when I approached my end days, and I considered my time spent with King Solomon as the happiest time of my life.

King Solomon explained to me a universal truth about life and my future. He said, "Life is the same as a beat of a heart, constantly vacillating between the two states of expansion and contraction." In contraction, our hearts are being constricted. When our hearts are open and in a state of expansion, we are free-flowing and open. Life always follows this pattern.

He explained that this was a parallel to my time in the graveyard. The graveyard was about hard labor and proving myself as a leader, which was a time of contraction. It was necessary for me to have experienced it fully so that I could appreciate the present moment. My expansion was living in the finest palace in the world and having a prophet and king as a trusted companion.

My life was changing, and I received an invitation to live in the royal palace with my friend, King Solomon. This is how a tough graveyard cat came to live among the elite of Jerusalem.

2.3 THE MERCHANT

There were many jewels in the palace of King Solomon, with him the biggest treasure of all. I was surrounded by luxuries and had my own quarters. It was challenging for me to adjust. The majority of the time, I chose to stay in my cat form while living in the palace. I was elevated to a position far above any household domestic pet. King Solomon had honored me by inviting me into his circle, and he demonstrated this by having a pillow for me placed next to his throne. I returned his friendship in the form of loyalty and a sense of responsibility to tell the truth and use a good sense of judgement, both of which I naturally excelled at.

On Saturdays, he held his lessons with the elite of Jerusalem, who would come sit with him in the garden. They learned about their true nature and how to improve their relationship with God. On Sundays, he held an open forum in his throne room, allowing those who had private questions to approach him. He would exercise his wisdom and implement the previous day's lesson. Seeing him in action was always exhilarating.

One Sunday, the merchant visited. It was the same merchant that King Solomon had saved me from. I sat on my cushion next to the throne, and the merchant recognized me. He understood that I wasn't just a domestic cat, although he hadn't approached me since the first day in the garden. His appearance had changed. He had lost a significant amount of weight, and it was clear that he was riddled with worry. He was so visibly agitated that even I could see he carried a heavy burden.

When the doors closed, his audience started with King Solomon and his court. He began to stutter, unable to produce words clearly, then he took a deep breath.

He said, "My King, I am deeply troubled."

King Solomon asked, "What troubles you?"

He explained, "I have difficulty sleeping."

King Solomon coaxed him, "Why?"

The merchant hesitated and looked at the few people in the room.

He said, "I dream I am in my bedroom trying on my finest robes when there is a knock on the door." Reluctantly, he continued, "When I answer the door no one is there, so I return to keep looking at my new clothes. When I am dressed and happy with my appearance, I look into the mirror one final time and see," his voice wavers, "that instead of my reflection, Death stares at me. I become paralysed. I fall to the floor, and I slowly lose my life. After this, I wake up."

King Solomon listened quietly. Dreams are omens, and King Solomon and I both knew that the dream meant the merchant was nearing the end of his life. The Merchant knew this also, but he came to King Solomon for confirmation.

King Solomon responded, "I see."

The room was tense, and we stared at the merchant visibly shaking in his boots.

The merchant said, "This is a reoccurring nightmare. My wife sent me to you, is it a sign?"

The merchant, his wife, King Solomon and I all knew it was a sign to be taken seriously. It was a message to warn the merchant to clean up any loose ends and to prepare his will and himself for his afterlife.

A knock was heard on the door. Strangely, King Solomon gestured for the stateroom doors to be opened, and a handsome man walked in. His clothes were not from our culture or time. It was highly unusual for an intimate audience to be interrupted in this fashion.

The handsome man approached King Solomon with a paper in his hand while he stared at the merchant critically. He had a brief interaction with King Solomon, but didn't take his eyes off the merchant. This was unusual as well because King Solomon normally held the attention of his visitors. The whole scene was very uncomfortable. The handsome man concluded his business and left the room.

The merchant radiated discomfort, and we all felt it. He was visibly disturbed by the presence of this man.

"Who was he, wise King?" the merchant asks in a shaking voice.

"That was Azrael," King Solomon replied matter-of-factly.

Azrael was the Angel of Death who often called on King Solomon. He was normally unseen and unheard by humans. King Solomon and I looked at each other as we realized that the merchant could see Azrael. It was an indication that the merchant was very close to the end of his days, far closer than we had thought.

"My King, I am scared. I saw him looking at me as if he wants me," said the merchant in a humble voice. "Please, you must do something to help me!" he beseeched his king and prophet.

King Solomon and I knew this was futile. The merchant would soon be met by Azrael, and nothing he could do would change this fact. King Solomon did not react to his request, but he understood that it was natural to be scared of death.

Thoughtfully, King Solomon offered, "So what do you want?"

The merchant pleaded, "I want you to save me from him by ordering the winds to carry me to the farthest part of India."

King Solomon rose from his throne and walked toward the open balcony that overlooked the palace gardens. He stood and whistled to the winds. Raising his hands as if conducting an orchestra, he whispered into the wind.

He said to the merchant, "Come here and the winds will carry you far away."

The merchant ran forward and stood with King Solomon on the balcony. The winds whipped through the trees and formed a small, compact tornado that encircled the merchant. The winds picked him up off the ground, and the merchant was carried from the floor of the throne room over the balcony and into the gardens. He was carried away as we all watched, and the Merchant was soon a dot on the horizon. After the merchant had disappeared, we all returned to our seats.

King Solomon returned to his throne, and he said to me, "That was very strange!"

As he settled, another knock was heard on the door. The door opened, and Azrael came back into the room with another paper for King Solomon.

King Solomon took the opportunity to ask, "Azrael, I saw you looking closely at one of my companions. Why did you stare at that man?"

Azrael answered, "Yes, indeed. I was surprised to see him here with you, beloved of God."

King Solomon asked, "Why were you so shocked?"

Azrael explained, "My instructions were to collect his spirit from the farthest part of India shortly after concluding business with you, and so I was astonished to see him standing here in your court."

King Solomon and I looked at each other, and we understood God's plan. King Solomon had sent the merchant to India, and this was where Azrael will collect him. The merchant's time of death would be soon, and there was a profound lesson to be learned: no one can escape death.

King Solomon dismissed Azrael, and we knew where he would be going. I felt blessed to witness this, as it helped me prepare for my own end.

2.4 THE HOOPOE

It was customary that every species of bird would present themselves to King Solomon for inspection every morning. One morning, the Hoopoe bird was missing from the lineup. King Solomon noticed immediately and was furious that the bird had left without permission. It was rare for any bird to waste its chance to spend time with King Solomon, and it was even more uncommon to defy him. When the Hoopoe bird returned to the palace, it was told to prepare for an audience with King Solomon to explain why it had gone missing without permission.

It was unclear if his absence was a sign of rebellion, which is the question we were all asking ourselves.

The Hoopoe was known to be an intelligent bird. On its return, it approached with caution. "My King. I was inspired last night to fly south. On my journey, I traveled into territories unknown."

We listened intently as the Hoopoe began its justification. We knew this situation was a matter of life or death for him.

He continued to explain, "What I tell you is the truth. I found people who were led by a queen. She has been granted many gifts from God, and she has a majestic throne. She and her people worship the sun, and Satan has tricked them and moved them away from the worship of one creator. They are happy with their deeds, but their eyes do not see the path, so they receive no guidance."

I thought the Hoopoe was telling the truth, and this was a serious matter for consideration. The occurrence had a significant meaning, and

King Solomon was mindful of his duties as a prophet before being a king. His job was to actively call all of creation to the worship of one creator. King Solomon was primarily a messenger. He was visibly troubled by the news that a queen had split the essence of the creator and encouraged the worship of individual aspects.

The Hoopoe said, "We could easily conquer her land. She has lots of gold and silver, and no army."

This was interesting, and aggression was a potential solution that would increase the wealth of King Solomon, but I knew King Solomon better than the Hoopoe did—I knew this would not be his preferred action. If there was no army, then their people had no reason to fight. I knew it troubled King Solomon that a small part of the Earth was not in submission to God, and this would be the motivation behind the decisions that King Solomon made.

King Solomon sent the Hoopoe back with an invitation tied to his wing. He flew to the palace of Sheba to summon Queen Bilkis to King Solomon. The message asked her to visit him to pay tribute to him, as did the other kings and queens of the world. If King Solomon's invitation were rejected, there would be a high price to pay.

A few months after this incident, the Hoopoe returned with a letter from Queen Bilkis, who had decided to visit King Solomon even though she had heard nothing of his reputation. She stated that although the journey typically took over seven years from Ethiopia to Jerusalem by land, she would try to come in three. Her letter was followed by a tribute of six thousand young people who were sent as slaves to King Solomon as a gift from her. As a prophet, King Solomon freed them on their arrival, thereby nullifying her gift.

Although times were tense, these actions gave us all hope for a peaceful resolution.

Years passed, and we heard news of Queen Bilkis being in our lands as she traveled to Jerusalem. A few days before we expected her, King Solomon was in his study. I could see he had something on his mind as he rummaged through drawers. He had a plan, and I asked him what is was.

"I'd like to bring the Queen's throne here, so she can sit on it while she visits," explained King Solomon.

It was not a small gesture, and I felt it would surely be appreciated, as it demonstrated that King Solomon wanted the queen to feel comfortable in the palace. Furthermore, it was a display of might, which would impress her.

You may wonder why I believed it would impress her.

Although she had officially been summoned to visit King Solomon to pay tribute, having her throne present recognised her sovereignty as a queen. Even if she did not believe in our creator, it was an attempt not to belittle her and her beliefs. I thought it was genius. However, I was curious as to how the throne would get to the palace.

"How do you intend to bring it here?" I asked.

After King Solomon rummaged around in his bureau, he found what he had been looking for: strands of hair. The hair belonged to the Afreet jinn who wanted to be of service to King Solomon. They had given him their hair so that he could call them if needed. They were among the most powerful of all the jinn, and I knew King Solomon intended to call them. One by one, he burnt the strands of hair in the flame of a nearby candle, summoning the jinn. These jinn had a reputation, and they were the ones that humans should have feared. I was a logical being—even I was scared of them because they were far superior to me in strength. They could be unstoppable. They knew they had been summoned to a private audience. King Solomon discussed the situation with the queen, and asked which jinni would be the one to bring her throne.

The strongest jinni stepped forward. This Afreet jinni had previously been so active in creating misguidance for mankind that since submitting to God and King Solomon's teachings, he still felt the need to prove his loyalty. He saw this as an opportunity to reinforce his loyalty and to compensate for his previous wrongdoings. The jinni immediately offered to bring the throne of the Queen of Sheba to the palace of King Solomon.

The throne was in front of us in the blink of an eye, and King Solomon asked for it to be placed next to his in the throne room. He then asked for its appearance to be altered, as he wanted to see if the queen would be aware that this was her throne.

The only job left was to wait for her arrival.

2.5 BILKIS THE QUEEN OF SHEBA

She was welcomed into Jerusalem with much pomp and splendor, befitting her status of a visiting queen. She was a handsome woman from the lands of Ethiopia. Her skin color was a deep and beautiful caramel. She had delicate, yet noble features. I knew that the meeting of Queen Bilkis and King Solomon would make history.

She was led into the throne room of King Solomon and presented to the king. She seemed genuinely happy to make his acquaintance. She clearly seemed to recognize the throne beside the king, but it was not the throne of her ancestors, which she had left behind. It was a glorious wooden throne embellished with jewels, gold, and ivory.

As delighted as she was to meet King Solomon, she could not keep from staring at the throne. Seeing her so distracted, King Solomon decided to reveal that this was her throne. He explained that the jinni brought her throne to his palace. She looked astonished as the jinni were commanded to reform the throne into its original shape and design. After the jinni had finished, she took her seat on her ancestral throne. Her throne was purposefully positioned next to King Solomon's so that she would not sit in a position of subjugation; it confirmed her status as his guest.

Queen Bilkis understood from this act that King Solomon was a powerful man, one who had more power than anyone she had met—including Bilkis herself. She had left her castle defended by a newly formed army, and still her throne had ended up in his palace. The queen knew she was dealing with a very unusual man, and I was sure she was in awe of his gifts, which would create loyalty in any human.

Her quest to visit him was to understand him, not as a king or ruler, but because she was intrigued by what she had heard of his status as prophet since entering his lands. On this point, she had made extensive enquiries into the man she had pledged to visit. King Solomon knew the real measure of whether she would submit herself to God would be after she had measured him on his wisdom and his Prophethood—not on displays of might and power. He was glad she valued wisdom in thought over displays of power.

Keen to understand more of King Solomon's wisdom, she asked him three riddles. She had prepared these riddles in advance with her council of advisors. They were the test she intended to use to see if she would pledge herself, her kingdom, and her people to King Solomon's God, and give up worship of the sun.

She asked her first riddle: "What is the ugliest thing in the world? And what is the most beautiful? What is the most certain? And what is the most uncertain?"

King Solomon answered this riddle with ease. "The ugliest thing in the world is a faithful person becoming unfaithful; the most beautiful thing in the world is the repentance of a sinner. The most certain thing in the world is death; the most uncertain thing in the world is how you will fare in the afterlife."

Queen Bilkis was satisfied by the answers that King Solomon had given her. She had used these questions to ascertain the measure of his knowledge, and she understood she was dealing with a prophet at this point. She seemed to have no question in her mind, but she wanted to make sure by asking the other two riddles.

King Solomon was patient, and he knew that for Queen Bilkis to declare her faith in God, he would need to be patient until she was ready. After all, he understood that faith in its highest form should have no compulsion.

Queen Bilkis asked her second riddle: "What is it that in a storm at sea goes ahead of all, is the cause of praise for the wealthy, of shame for the poor, honors the dead and saddens the living, is a joy to the birds and causes grief to the fish?"

King Solomon smiled. He knew the answer, and with each riddle, he knew he was faring better in her evaluation.

"Flax," he said. "When woven into cloth, it makes a sail for the ship, fine clothes for the rich and rags for the poor, and shrouds for the dead. The birds delight in its seed, and the fish are caught in its net."

Queen Bilkis said, "Yes, that is correct."

Her surety in King Solomon grew with each riddle. She asked him her final riddle as the entire court sat and watched the meeting of two immensely powerful people.

Queen Bilkis asked, "What land is that which has but once seen the sun?"

King Solomon answered, "The land upon which, after the creation, the waters were gathered."

The speed of King Solomon's responses convinced her of the king's wisdom. Wisdom was an essential ingredient in prophecy, and the meeting was proving promising. The court disbanded for the night, and I went to observe the queen in private. I wanted to see if she was thinking over the events of the day, and when I was satisfied, I would dissolve into the shadows to let her rest.

When Queen Bilkis retired to her bedchamber that night, she called for a wise advisor who was part of her entourage. Together, they considered what she had seen. They agreed that King Solomon had great wisdom because he knew the answers to all the riddles she had put before him, and he was a gifted man. He could control the animals and had command of the jinn. She knew she was dealing with a man the likes of which she had never encountered before. Her advisor mentioned that prophets were not like typical people. He reminded her that she had offered him tribute in the form of slaves, and he had rejected them by setting them free. They both knew that King Solomon's will could not be purchased. The queen said that she knew that King Solomon only wanted one thing.

When her advisor asked what this one thing was, she answered that King Solomon wanted her submission to God, and she would use her time with him to evaluate him and what he was calling her toward. She confessed that she would likely accept his God within her heart; after all, the sun set, so maybe it was foolish to worship it. The advisor left her chambers, and I dissolved from her room knowing what was in her heart.

The next morning, she had a breakfast of the most amazing figs and honey with the ripest tomatoes, olives, and pomegranates, and a variety of cheeses.

After breakfast, she was summoned to meet with King Solomon in a great hall. When the doors opened, she was astounded. In front of her, a glass castle shone brightly, captivating her eyes. There was a glass path leading up to it. Glass had not yet been invented in our age, so it appeared awesome to her. Water ran under the glass, and she fully expected to get wet. She stepped onto the glass with her skirts raised with wonder and trepidation, her mind unable to process what her eyes were seeing.

King Solomon realized what she thought and said, "Queen Bilkis, your clothes will not get wet."

It was a statement made to protect her modesty, and as she stood on the glass, she could see that the water ran underneath it and not over it. She dropped her skirt and wondered at the miraculous material.

The glass was a wonder. She had no idea that glass existed, and she saw that it was a miracle of God, which had to be recognised.

After deep reflection and soul searching following this meeting, Queen Bilkis acknowledged that the sun, which she had worshiped, was just a sign of God and not God Himself.

It was not long after this that she accepted the God of King Solomon and King Solomon himself as her prophet, as did her people.

For me, my journey had noticed the pious people of the grave, and now the entire earth was filled with remembrance of its creator. It was a truly momentous occasion to have Queen Bilkis visit, and it was proof that King Solomon had accomplished his goals as a prophet.

Living in the royal palace and being a first-hand witness to these events only brought me closer to King Solomon and the word of God. He was a man I had enjoyed spending time with, a man I truly loved. It was my death that caused us to part, and he followed a few short months later.

Mr Time

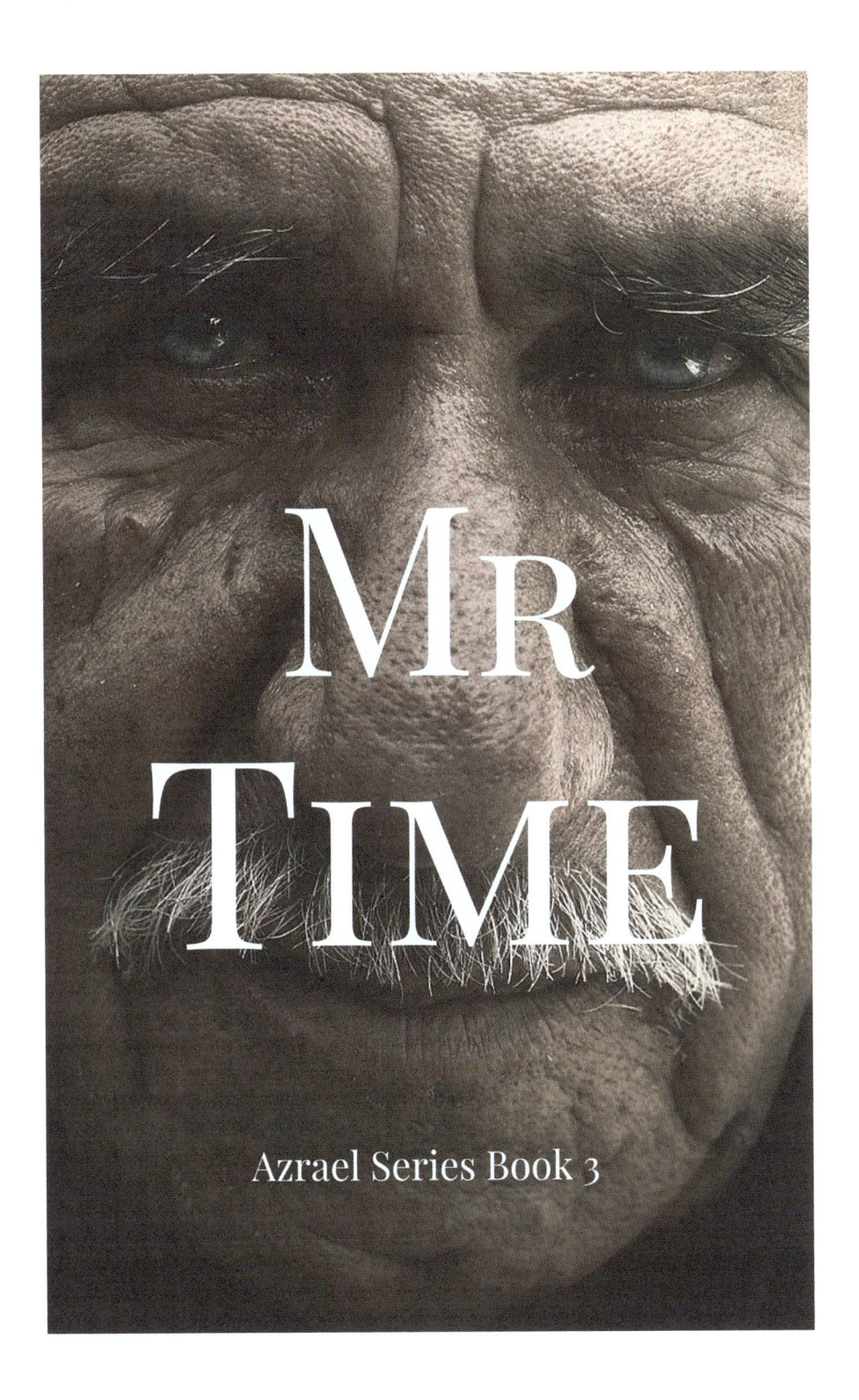

Azrael Series Book 3

3.1 THE COUNTDOWN

She never noticed his burning, sapphire eyes. His eyes held the wisdom and knowledge of life for over ninety-five years. He was a man who knew many secrets. He did not have a humble, insignificant life, but one of spirituality, strategy, family, love, service, and statesmanship. His life story had seen the fall of two grand empires, and in his time, he witnessed the essence of what made a man a human being.

The nurse couldn't see past the fact that he had soiled himself again. She chided him for what he had done.

"I suppose I have to clean you up," she said with a huff and a wrinkled nose.

He did not respond to her acrid tone, as he knew it was her job—a job for which his children paid her nursing home bosses handsomely. He did not even know her name. She had no idea how significant she was to him: she was his only connection to the living.

In the curse of old age, he discovered that his children had abandoned him. They were lost to an ideal of the family being a small nuclear unit and to a consumerist mentality, which, in its extreme, included disposable people. He was a victim of their modern ideology. Preoccupied with their ideals, they conveniently forgot him in a nursing home. They paid to get rid of their problem. Behavior such as this was unheard of fifty years ago. It was understood that because a father raised his son in his tender years, the son would protect and serve his father in his later years. This was the natural cycle of life. This man knew better than to impose his historic ideals on his only son who still lived in England with him. All his other children had left the country to chase dreams around the world, and the distance between them grew. He accepted that his life was based in the past, and he could not push his children to view the world from his perspective.

The nurse knew nothing of the vulnerability and loneliness he felt, and every day, he experienced her growing contempt for him. Theirs was a love-hate relationship: in his own way, he loved her, and she grew a little seed of hate for him in her heart.

She left the room, and he knew she would come back before the end of her shift. She would let him sit in his feces until then, his nose assaulted by the smell. Later, she would come back to strip the bedding—and him of his last ounce of dignity. This was fast becoming their nightly routine.

He felt triumphant sitting in his own excrement. She would come back. As she left the room, he smiled wryly knowing that he would have more time with this objectionable woman. He smiled because she was another human being to spend time with.

His family had dumped him here because they believed that he was losing his faculties. Maybe they were right. Although this theory neglected to mention that his daughter-in-law had discovered that he thought she was a mean-hearted woman because she had secretly listened to his private telephone conversation. As a result, he had ended up in the nursing home with increasingly rare visits from his son, in his fifties and still not a man. The grandchildren stopped coming altogether, each busy with different classes and sports. His complaints were purposefully superficial, as they masked the fact that his heart was broken.

His son loved his mother more than Mr. Time. It was natural for mothers and sons to be close, which any anthropologist will say is the root of the daughter-in-law and mother-in-law conflict. His wife and son's relationship wasn't something Mr. Time felt the need to compete with, but he wished his son saw value in him, too.

Vain wishes aside, he knew he had lived a full life, typical of a man with great wisdom. He could guess a person's character from a hundred yards based on their interactions, behaviors, and gestures. These were the essence of a man.

Character was the single most valuable asset a man could possess in the world, and Mr. Time knew character was based on how a man had been raised. A good family was fundamental to developing a great and productive society, and he had a great example in his own father. In his elderly state, he longed to feel the cool touch of his fathers' hand against his skin. The blessing of having parents was that you knew everything would be all right. Parents offered stability.

As Mr. Time sat in his dark room awaiting the return of the nurse, he longed for those he had lost over his long life. The longing overwhelmed him, and tears ran down his leathery cheeks. He was fighting to stay in the world of the living—or was it that he had no choice at this particular moment? He knew he did not belong in this era of constant connectedness, fast talking, and multiscreen watching. He longed for the end, but this terrified him, too.

Should he pursue his will to live? Was living really that important? He was ninety-five and filled with pain; he had nothing other than Death to look forward to. The next question he always asked himself was whether he was ready. He didn't know the answer. Ninety-five was a blessing, as it had given him ample time to assess his life and be grateful for it. He felt more fortunate than those who had lost their lives at earlier ages, but what did that mean for him? He knew that achieving an age like this meant bidding goodbye to everyone, and he had. Everyone was gone. Only the nurse was left.

He wasn't a man built to be lonely. He had always craved company and actively sought the companionship of the most powerful men who moved and shook the world. Sitting in his bed now, he had become the thing he feared: an insignificant old man who regularly soiled himself. His awareness came back to his present state, and he begged his Creator to accept him into the next life, the next stage of existence. He sorely missed his wife, his friends, his brothers and sisters, his parents, and friends. Everyone was gone.

The first inkling that this prayer might have been accepted was when the nurse returned to the room. She stripped him naked and removed the sheets from the bed. She moved her wet cloth in between his creases and wiped him down. In his vulnerable state, he pondered the fact that he was a shell of the man he had once been: his leathered skin hollow where muscle used to be, his brittle nails, his white hair, and the smell of old age clinging to his body like a cheap cologne. His declining state made his prayer more intense.

She had changed him, but he felt more disconnected from her than he ever had. His change is attitude to his only companion should have been his first clue. When she finished, she flicked off the light, but a small, white light entered the room and hovered at the corner above the door, like a small torch. The nurse left the room unaware of the light, and then Mr. Time knew that he wasn't alone anymore.

He smiled. The nurse thought it was due to the care she had shown him. She was unused to him acknowledging her, and she left him feeling that maybe in the future she would have more patience with him. A glimmer of compassion entered her heart and started to eat away at the bitterness.

3.2 THE DREAM

The light stayed in the corner of the room awaiting the departure of the nurse before coming closer to Mr. Time. He could see it because his Creator often allowed him to perceive more than the ordinary man; Mr. Time was sensitive to the paranormal. The light flew around his feet in a circular motion, moving up his body until it was finally around his head. It was as if the light was scanning him, akin to a medical procedure. It felt as if a hair dryer had just blown hot air against his face. A change of winds set in motion, and he knew the light signified an end to his earthly existence. The light stayed with him until he fell into a deep, restful slumber. His dream state showed him his wife and younger sister sitting together in a flowery meadow. They played with the various flowers and fauna. They laughed and enjoyed each other's company. Mr. Time marveled at how healthy they looked. They were so free, so alive, so young. They welcomed him to sit with them, and they told him they were waiting for him.

He hadn't seen their faces for an eternity, and he missed them with an intense longing. When he tried to recall their faces while he was awake, he could only remember features, not their full faces. It had frustrated him that he could not visualize them fully. He always remembered their energy and love. Seeing them again in their youth, he longed to join them as soon as possible. His wife, Khadija (whom he nicknamed Khadi), told him that they would see him soon. The dream ended with this fortuitous news, and he knew it signified that the countdown had begun. Mr. Time woke with a vigorous mind and the same withered body.

Mr. Time had learned to interpret dreams at an early age. He knew this auspicious dream meant that he was now in the last forty days of his life. His father, who had been his spiritual teacher, had told him that when a man is in his final forty days, you could look at him with your *aynul basera* (your inner spiritual eye) to see a man withering and becoming dry like a plant. Mr. Time felt a sense of excitement at the thought of being with those he loved, and the journey ahead gave finality to his life—and what a life he had seen.

His father had been his second teacher after his mother, and his father had been the single biggest influence over his life. The village *Imam* (clergyman), his father had a reputation among the local Muslim and Hindu population as one who was truthful. His father was loved, respected, and feared so much that even the local Hindus came to him for advice and guidance. Mr. Time took his spirit and sense of justice from his father.

His mother had been heartbroken when her children left their village, but she was a real woman, and she knew to put the betterment of her children before herself. She was a woman who understood the meaning of raising children with character. She was a strong woman of principle who served her family and was a role model for the community. Mr. Time's parents had done so much for their community; they were truthful, respected, rightful, and knowledgeable people. It didn't take a huge leap of imagination to understand that their lives were the microcosm and Mr. Time's existence was the macrocosm.

He adopted his parents' ideals and turned them into his philosophy, and this journey had resulted in him being recognized under the British Raj and given a prestigious job of Chief Magistrate for the region. The British knew they could trust his scrupulous character—even more than their people. He was recognized in all of India and later Pakistan. His name was both revered and feared. Later in life, he represented the UN as a foreign envoy to other countries, which meant he traveled the world and, as a result, he knew many of its people.

Mr. Time was by no means a small thinker. He was a man built for greatness. The essence of his training from an early age was to see potential and opportunity. His career was illustrious, and anyone he thought well of was given a position of responsibility and a wage that allowed them to be real providers for their families. He changed and touched the lives of all of his family and inspired his brothers and cousins to push and excel.

When of a marriageable age, his mother received much interest. All the local women understood that marriage to Mr. Time would mean their daughters' lives, and by extension their lives, would be made. He had the pick of any woman in the community, but unlike many others, he chose to marry for love. It was a match his mother and father tacitly disapproved of, but they never voiced their dislike. They implemented their own advice to adapt and accept their new daughter-in-law Khadija, and they prayed for the happy couple to be blessed with children. Mr. Time and Khadija had five sons and two daughters, all of who went on to achieve greatness in their own ilk. He had risen from a mud village in India to state dinners with the Queen of England.

All this meant nothing. The highs of his life were similar to the lows, and he had bitter disappointments, too. He knew the human character inside and out. He knew the depths it could reach. He witnessed the partition of India at an early age and saw the brutality and savagery of men who gave into their lower natures. They could be responsible for such death and destruction. He also knew his Creator was watching him, so he strived to actively choose the correct and righteous path.

He was glad to be ending his life in this world, but he was also afraid. He knew that while he sat in his room in seclusion from the rest of the world, he would have many visitors, family and friends from non-worldly realms, in the next forty days to help him prepare for the transition.

He kept his Qur'an by his bedside and his *Tashbih* (prayer beads) in his hand. He awaited his visitors and tried to recount the dead he wanted to see. All of these thoughts took him further from the earthly dimension. As he fell asleep, he welcomed visitors in his heart.

Majeed entered his father's room, hovering over him to check his pulse.

Mr. Time said, "Majeed, is that you?"

"*Assalaamalikum* (peace be upon you), *Baba* (Dad)," Majeed replied. His eyes were dark and sunken, and his skin was ashen. He had aged since Mr. Time had seen him last.

"*Walikum salaam* (Peace be with you also)," Mr. Time said, anxious that the living were visiting and not the dead as he had expected.

"What are you doing here?" Mr. Time was curious as to why his son was visiting on a workday.

Majeed, reassured that his father was still alive, pulled up a chair next to his father's bed.

"Baba, I had a strange dream last night. I saw Mum, and she asked me to visit you," Majeed confessed. "I was worried!"

Mr. Time smiled, genuinely happy to see his son—the same son who hadn't visited for over six months. He was happy to know that the strong son and mum connection didn't cease even from the grave, and he was reminded that his wife had always been fantastic at multitasking. Trying to reassure his son was his immediate priority, but he was conflicted. He knew that the secrets that had been shared with him about his final moments could not be divulged.

Mr. Time began by consoling his son. "Son, don't worry. I'm an old man. For me, it is only a matter or time." He knew he sounded reasonable and that he must pretend that the wheels had not been set in motion. He knew Majeed would only worry, and as a father, it was his instinct to protect his child without lying to him.

Majeed had heard his father say that it was just a matter of time for many years. It was the truth for every living being, but the familiar statement that masked the excitement in Mr. Time's eyes was a comfort to Majeed.

Had Majeed been spiritually aware, he would have seen that his father was in the last forty days of his life. Majeed had come for comfort, and Mr. Time supplied it.

Majeed chattered inanely about his children, his wife, upcoming holidays, and his in-laws. Mr. Time dutifully nodded at the right cues. Mr. Time was touched by his son's visits and knew it was likely the last time he would see Majeed. He was glad that his son lived a full life and that he wasn't a burden on him. He used to feel disappointed in Majeed, an inner feeling that he had never communicated to Majeed or even Khadija. The cause of this was Majeed's relaxed attitude toward performing service for his parents. He burdened his parents in their old age with his worries, his debts, and worst of all, his temper.

As his son chatted like an old village woman, Mr. Time knew for the first time that his son's shortcomings were not due to a lack of parenting, but because his son was, in many ways, a selfish boy. Mr. Time felt free of the deficiencies of Majeed. He watched his son chit-chat away, and he waited patiently for him to leave. Mr. Time appreciated that his loneliness gave him freedom and peace.

Mr. Time eventually fell asleep while Majeed spoke, as was the habit of elderly folk. In his dream state, he felt Majeed prepare to leave his side.

Majeed gave him a warm kiss on his forehead and asked him for forgiveness for his shortcomings. Majeed also asked his father to make all the wrongdoing of the past *halal* (acceptable) and to have all the rights he had taken made *haqq* (rightful). Mr. Time had not heard his son speak like this before. Momentarily, he thought he might have misjudged his son. He was unsure if his son was truly aware that the next time he would see his father would likely be at his funeral prayer.

In his dream, Khadija told him that he should not be so harsh on Majeed and that he was a decent son deep down. The times when Majeed had used his temper to intimidate his father into submission made Mr. Time uncertain that his wife was a good judge of character regarding their son. He felt she was blinded by her love for her children. He could not easily forgive his son for his past behaviors, and he reserved judgement on whether he would grant his son these two rights. Khadija thought he was being extreme. Bickering with his wife from beyond the grave, Mr. Time marveled at the way his deceased wife could meddle. He was glad to see her, and he was sure he would be seeing her more often as the days passed. That thought excited him. With Khadija, he would be able to resume a normal life, a familiar existence. He started to relive the days that had passed.

As time progressed and the forty days ticked away, Mr. Time frequently sat on his bed alone, having conversations in hushed tones. His dead family members came to visit him in dreams and also in his waking state. His bedroom had become a place of laughter, where he reconnected with his family and spent time in what his nurse bleakly thought was a fantasy world. He was busying himself with the people he loved, and he relived old times with them as they came to visit him. He was preparing to cross over to the other side.

He left the chair in place next to the bed, and a new guest was waiting to speak with him each time he woke. He reminisced about the past, about the funny and sad things that had happened. Memories of his childhood and his brothers and sisters came flooding back. He would be with them soon.

His loneliness disappeared as the people from the grave came to pay their respects to him. He was not alone. He had company during the day and during his dreams, all with the great promise that he would soon be with the people he loved.

Mr. Time grew to accept his death, and he knew that was the purpose of the otherworldly visitors. He also knew he was blessed to be facing the opportunity to enter Heaven. Yes, it was a huge presumption, but, similar to saints, he had been blessed to know his end date. He could prepare. Mr. Time knew that the prospect of a future in Hell was a less likely outcome for him. He did not fear Hell. His only fear had been displeasing his Creator. He also understood the fiery torment was similar to a headmasters' cane, a deterrent to doing anything that the Creator would not consider acceptable. The rules on acceptable and unacceptable were very clear.

He had fallen asleep again at dinner and this time, the nurse woke him. He had started to skip meals, and he looked noticeably weaker. She had heard him laughing alone in his room, and she often checked on him. He was usually sleeping, and sometimes she heard multiple voices from his room even though no one was there. At this point, even she could see the signs. She knew that Mr. Time was coming to an end. Being around the elderly meant being around death, and even she was familiar with its signs.

3.3 AZRAEL

When he awoke, he expected Khadija to be sitting on the chair. She normally vanished from his dreams to sit with him while he was awake. He opened his eyes and looked immediately at the chair by his bed.

A man sat in the chair. Mr. Time wiped the sleep away from his eyes as he willed his eyes to focus. It took him a little while to realize that the man sitting with him was not a family member and not a face he had seen before.

His eyes focused. The man sitting with him was young, handsome, stocky, and strong. He wore an incredible perfume, the smell of which filled the room and delighted Mr. Time's nose. As he saw Mr. Time wake up, the man smiled. There was a kindness in his eyes, and he looked like a perfect gentleman. Mr. Time, frantic not to be rude, searched his memory for a clue to the man's identity. After a few moments of not speaking, Mr. Time realised that he did, in fact, know and expect him. This man was Azrael. He was glad he had received a visit like this. Azrael sat with him patiently. He hoped this was an auspicious sign and that this meant his final judgement would be good. The visit gave Mr. Time hope.

Azrael the archangel did not seem hurried. He sat in the chair with a reassuring presence.

"*Salaam* (peace)," said Mr. Time to acknowledge Azrael.

"*Walikum salaam*," responded Azrael, returning the customary greeting of mutual peace. "Do you know who I am?" Azrael asked curiously.

Mr. Time nodded, not wanting to say the name he had whispered in reverence for so many years. "Welcome. I have been expecting you, and I am glad to meet you," said Mr. Time. "It's not been a full forty days as yet. Have you come to take me early?"

Azrael shook his head, "My purpose is to inform you that I will take you after three days. You have a little time to get your affairs in order."

Mr. Time calculated which day he would die. It would be on Thursday, which he hoped meant that his funeral prayer would be after the Friday midday prayer and that his body would be committed to soil on Friday. He hoped his son would be free to wash his body, as was the custom. He did not want a stranger touching his body because he feared a stranger would not treat his dead body with dignity.

Azrael added, "Prepare as much as you can."

As Mr. Time reflected, he considered for the first time the pangs of death that he knew he would feel. As a vulnerable old man, he was concerned with the level of physical pain he would endure. This thought frightened him. At his age, a cold breeze could do damage, so death was a severe concern.

"Do you know what will happen next?" Azrael asked with a kindness that Mr. Time had never associated with him. Mr. Time knew, but stayed silent. He wanted to be reminded. He wanted to learn the process of the journey from Azrael directly. Mr. Time sat comfortably and gave Azrael his full attention. He needed to understand how he could become one with his family again.

Azrael told him that his body was like a dead seed that would be planted in the ground. From it, his discipline in worship that he had demonstrated during his life would grow like roots to anchor him in the soil. His good actions would form shoots, which would break through the surface of the ground and provide sustenance in the form of fruit to others.

Azrael knew that as a spiritual man, Mr. Time had impacted the lives of many people positively, helping people nurture their relationships with their Creator. Azrael shared with him an understanding of death, but he knew Mr. Time wanted to know about the process.

"Clearly, there will be pain," said Azrael. "When the time comes, your body will be separated from your spirit. This will be painful."

He continued to describe the numbing of the toes that would spread up the shins and calves, through the limbs, and finally, into the heart as the spirit was removed from the body. The heart is the seat of the spirit. The physical heart holds this significance. The severity of the pain would at some point cut off the heart and tongue from expressing themselves. If Mr. Time had strength left, it would manifest in the death rattle, which would be the last sounds he made as his spirit and body were separated and the gate of repentance was closed. His skin color would turn to an ashy gray, reflecting the dust from which it was created. His tongue would be pulled back at the root and swell in his mouth to fill it and push his mouth open. His eyes would roll up to the tops of their sockets as they watched the soul exit the body. His fingertips would turn greenish black. Azrael told him it was normal to feel a sense of sorrow as he departed from his body, which had been his home.

The agony of death accounted for shortcomings in life and reflected a person's actions. For a man destined for Hell, an easy death is payback for any good done in his life. A man destined for Heaven was often in agony. This reminded Mr. Time of the passing of his Prophet Muhammed Rasul (SAW), who also had a painful death. This bolstered Mr. Time's confidence. A painful death would make him feel connected with his Prophet and Messenger, although he still feared the taste of death and the bitterness that his heart would feel during the process. Mr. Time knew he was right to fear death. A clever man could only fear death, and he made a silent prayer for a death that he could bear.

Azrael continued his account of the process of dying. After the pangs of death and the official meeting with Azrael, he would collect Mr. Time's soul. The next step was for the angels who record the life actions of men to show Mr. Time a run-through of his actions on Earth. These angels would either welcome Mr. Time or shun him. This depended on the final destination of the person.

Mr. Time was aware that although he was engaging in a cozy chat with Azrael, the reality was that he still had no clear idea of his final destination: Heaven or Hell? He feared for his soul and was concerned that he could have done more in his devotion or given more in charity. Had he been remiss or deficient in any way?

Sitting with Azrael and having a pre-meeting with him was not enough to guarantee a destiny in Heaven or a reunion with those he loved. Most of all, he loved his Creator and hoped that he would be a worthy enough servant to see his Creator's face.

Azrael knew what was on his mind. "Do not fear. You will not leave this Earth without knowing your final destination." He added, "I cannot reveal it to you now."

Although he was anxious about not knowing his outcome, Mr. Time knew he must submit to the wisdom of not knowing. He asked, "What can I do to ensure a positive outcome?"

Azrael answered, "Did Majeed ask something of you?"

Mr. Time cast his memory back and recalled his last meeting with his son. After a few moments, his son's voice asking for forgiveness sounded in his consciousness. He wanted to be stubborn and not forgive Majeed for his neglect. He could only compare his relationship with Majeed to his relationship with his father. He had doted on his elderly father, and his father had passed away with an entire village to mourn him. The death of his father was dignified.

Where was this for Mr. Time? Had he been forgotten? He had been shut out of sight in a nursing home. In his vulnerable state, he was treated as an inconvenience and a burden. He was useless and unhelpful. He had lost his ability to express himself as he lost his strength and bitterness had grown in his heart that was focused on his son. He felt he deserved more consideration and care; he was a man who was built to be involved in the family, not left to die alone! Mr. Time's old age bore no blessings as his father's had—it was a curse.

He knew that Azrael mentioned Majeed for good reason. Did he want to leave this Earth with malice and bitterness in his heart?

He wasn't sure if he could forgive Majeed, but he took Azrael's point. He accepted that maybe his relationship with the living was the reason death had not come earlier in his life. He knew Azrael was looking for acknowledgment of the question, so he said, "I need to think about it."

Azrael knew that Mr. Time needed time to consider the situation with his son. He also knew that this stubbornness was the smallest black spot in Mr. Time's heart. He wished that Mr. Time would truly leave this stubbornness, as it was an anchor in his heart that tied him to the Earthly dimension. The Creator did not want Mr. Time with this negativity in his heart, and in this regard, Mr. Time was deficient. Azrael knew the Creator had a plan.

They sat with each other in growing familiarity as Mr. Time, a decrepit old man with a partially hard heart, acknowledged that Azrael knew his deepest secrets.

"Tell me about the grave" Mr. Time said, eager to make the most of the opportunity with Azrael.

Azrael shared the mysteries of the afterlife. "The grave will have a direct relationship with your state. If your state is good, your grave will be good. If your state is bad, your grave will be bad. Death, in reality, is an alteration in state." Mr. Time looked thoughtful, and Azrael continued. "You have already entered the state of death, which is why your vision has changed. You can see beyond the existing light spectrum available to most human beings. You can see beings in other light frequencies beyond the ultraviolet and infrared. Death is the death of your body, but your soul will live on. Your soul is immortal, and it is your real nature."

Mr. Time knew this was the truth. Death was moments away.

Azrael continued his lesson. "When a man dies, he is deprived of his property, his family, his ability to use his body. It is this separation that causes pain. His soul will think of all the things that he owned and all the things in which he took pleasure. If he took pleasure in remembering his Creator, then the barriers between him and his Creator will be removed."

A smile crept onto Mr. Time's face, demonstrating that he understood this statement. He knew in his heart that he had tried all his life to remember his Creator in both the good and bad times, and he desperately hoped that his Creator was happy with him.

Azrael gave Mr. Time a hard look and said, "Do you know that people are asleep, and when they die, they wake up?"

Mr. Time nodded. He had heard this before. Azrael continued with his lesson. The first things to be revealed were your good and evil actions. The good benefits you in the afterlife, whereas the evil harms you. Everything you have done has been written down. Your soul will see your sins, which will make you miserable, and your soul will be your judge. This will all happen before your breath stops.

Once you are interred in the ground, your spirit may return to your body. If this happens, it will be to face chastisement for your behavior in this world.

Your soul is immortal, as is your intellect and knowledge. You will take all these things with you to the grave, where you will be reminded of your good and bad actions. The grave will either become a chasm of Hell or a garden of Heaven. The man who is successful in death is the one who knows he has sold his Earthly existence willingly for his afterlife. He has no attachment to this life or this world. He is a genuine lover of God, and he will get his heart's desire.

Mr. Time thought of the martyrs of the past, entering battle and willingly running toward their deaths for the love of their Creator. He hoped he could muster a similar sense of love for his Creator. He was jealous of these martyrs.

"You know the grave will speak with you," stated Azrael.

"What will it say?" asked Mr. Time.

"Your grave will ask you if you remembered him. If you contemplated him. And it will remind you that it is a house of tribulation and trial, a house of worms. Your good deeds will inform the grave that either you will be a resident in Heaven, at which point the grave will become amiable and garden-like, or you will be a resident of Hell, in which case the grave will become a prison."

These words scared Mr. Time as he thought about being put into a small space and being unable to move. With all his might and sincerity, he hoped for a positive outcome.

Again, Azrael knew what was on his mind. "If you have lived a righteous life, you will find your good acts, such as your charity, your prayer, your pilgrimage, your fasting, will provide you with comfort from the trials of the grave. If demons come to visit you and try to disturb your peace, your actions in this world will protect you from them."

Encouraged by this, Mr. Time listened carefully to the secrets of the afterlife that were being divulged.

Azrael continued, "If you are protected, angels will appear to place a cloth and a candle from Heaven in your grave. They will push the boundaries of your grave as far as your eyes can see, and you will have comfort until you are summoned for your judgement. Otherwise, they will ask the grave to constrict around your body, and you will be crushed by the Earth."

Shuddering at the thought of the punishment in the grave, Mr. Time hoped his soul could skip that part. Azrael was Mr. Time's teacher, and Mr. Time knew better than to interrupt his lesson. He let Azrael continue.

"Have you heard of Munkar and Nakir?" Azrael asked. Mr. Time gulped air, and beads of sweat formed on his brow. He knew those names. They were the tormentors of the grave, reported to have blue-black skin, voices like thunder, eyes like lightning, and hair that reached the ground. They were a fearful sight to behold. Mr. Time knew of them and was determined to hold his intellect against their questioning.

Sensing this, Azrael said, "They are two angels who will come to your grave to ask you three questions. You will know the answers." He paused.

Mr. Time took his cue and asked, "What are the three questions?"

Azrael said, "Oh Man! Who is your Lord?"

This was a trial run, and Mr. Time knew he must answer. Tentatively, he said, "My Lord is God."

Azrael nodded. "What is your religion?"

Mr. Time answered, "Islam."

Azrael nodded again. "Who is your Prophet?"

Mr. Time responded, "Muhammed, peace be upon him."

"These questions will be asked of you as soon as the last person attending your funeral is ten yards away from your grave. This is not a test you can cheat on." said Azrael.

Mr. Time thought carefully about how he needed to prepare, and Azrael had given him a clue that he needed to build bridges with Majeed. He thought about his son and what his son had asked of him. He needed to make it right. As he considered this, he looked at the chair, but it was empty. Azrael had gone. Mr. Time knew that he would only see him again when it was time.

3.4 FORGIVENESS

Mr. Time was concerned about his final destination. It was an auspicious sign to have coaching from Azrael, but the unresolved forgiveness asked for by Majeed weighed heavily on his mind.

Could he genuinely forgive his son for treating him this way? He had felt he had raised him as a good boy; he had done as much as a father could do. His son had attended the best schools. He had ensured he had an Islamic and a secular education. He had taught his children values. He had shared with his son what it took to be a good man and parent. His son had never wanted for anything.

He weighed up the pros and cons. He might have a better position in Heaven if he could get over the hard heart he had developed and genuinely forgive his son. Alternatively, if he never forgave his son, the Creator could judge between them on the day of judgement. It was his forgiveness to give, so why did it seem so hard?

After Azrael had left, Mr. Time was lonely for the first time in the forty days. Azrael was a tough act to follow, and he had a lot to consider. He didn't need to be distracted by the small talk of the people from the grave.

Did Majeed deserve forgiveness? Was he even a man? Majeed had been influenced by his wife and taken on a female villager mindset. Mr. Time hadn't been fond of his daughter-in-law, but he could not object to her being Majeed's wife—he had also chosen his own woman in Khadija.

Majeed's wife was inelegant, and her voice was shrill like a banshee. She was vulgar and spoke openly with the family about issues like inheritance and money. She had no endearing qualities, no breeding, and her poise was reflective of the rough village background of her bloodline. Mr. Time and Khadija did their best to welcome Majeed's wife into the fold of the family, but she was intent on making her presence felt. She was not a good daughter-in-law, and she could make herself feel unwelcome quickly. She was unable to roll with the flow of family life and therefore, many arguments ensued. Her temper made it difficult to remain civil.

After Khadija died, Majeed did the noble thing and invited his father to live with his family. He had, in fact, invited his father into a minor hell. Mr. Time initially enjoyed the company of Majeed's children and they enjoyed his as well, but Majeed's wife tried to limit their time together. Trying to think well of her, he reasoned it was due to the fact that he was an old man, and she wanted to give him a break. The children had soon lost interest in their grandfather, and they only seemed to be interested in their smartphones. For a short time, he tried to learn their computer language, but he gave up when they laughed at him. Yes, he had laughed along, but he knew he was not built for this age. He wanted a place that was warm and comfortable to pray, so when the care home was mentioned, he thought it could be an answer to his prayers.

The care home residents weren't Muslim like him. They were all old people waiting for their souls to be collected. He had nothing in common with them, so he sat alone on his bed for the majority of the day. The care home was chosen due to its proximity to Majeed's house, but this in itself was a joke. Majeed never visited. At first, he visited due to the guilt he felt for placing his father there, but after he grew comfortable with the guilt, he rarely visited.

All of this was a stark contrast to the life Mr. Time had led and the imbibed understanding of service for others, which was the mark of a profound depth of character. Mr. Time performed service for others. He had looked after others' interests and often placed other people before his individual interests. He knew about respecting the elderly and listening to them speak, and no one would have ever interrupted his father or considered raising their voice in his presence. He knew about service to the elderly, and the promise was that if you conduct service to the elderly, then your children will perform service for you. This was understood. It was a rule of nature as reliable as gravity.

Where had Majeed gone wrong?

Khadija came into the room and sat upon the bed. She said, "We need to talk."

Mr. Time sat with her and before she could jump to his Majeed's defense, Mr. Time said sorrowfully, "He left me here, Khadi." His eyes welled up with tears, and immediately he was a boy: lost, forsaken, and defenseless. He continued, "I'm his Dad! And he left me."

His tears wet the sheets where they landed. His tears give way to full-blown sobs. "So you're disappointed?" she asked him.

"I'm hurt, Khadi. That is worse than disappointed."

"Don't you think there are times when you disappointed him?" she asked. Mr. Time searched his memory and could think of nothing. He shook his head.

Khadija looked at him with pity. She said, "My love, your work was your life's biggest passion. Your career overshadowed us all. Majeed was the most sensitive of our children, and he needed you when you were at your state dinners. He learned to live without you from an early age. That is what you are feeling now."

As Khadija explained, Mr. Time fell deeper into despair. His wife's candid words got to the core of the issue. Mr. Time had been a great statesman and spiritual leader, continuously giving advice and guidance to others, always making himself available. He always felt that Khadija had domestic life covered. He hadn't considered the contribution to domesticity that he should have made. He had never noticed his deficiencies until this point; he had always felt Majeed was a difficult child looking for attention. He realized that he had always judged Majeed.

His tears stung, and his nose ran. It was too late. The dying process had opened his eyes. He prided himself on being able to tell a man's character, but he did not even know his own son.

Khadija touched his face when she could see that he was starting to see Majeed's perspective. Her otherworldly hand had the faintest feeling of warmth, but the familiarity made Mr. Time want to be with her.

She knew how he felt. "Soon, my love, we will be together. In the meantime, you need to consider what Majeed asked of you."

Mr. Time fell asleep two nights before his death with a heavy heart.

The dream was lucid, but he was used to them at this point. He had returned to his childhood, and his father was giving a lesson in the village. He sat and listened as he used to. His father was discussing how even a mustard seed of impurity in the heart could stop a believer from entering paradise. It was a lesson he had heard his father deliver many times, but this time, his father called him aside. They sat together on the wooden benches outside the old family home in India.

His father was his teacher, so it was appropriate that he raised the issue of Majeed. "Majeed's request. You've left the boy waiting a long time, nearly the full forty days," he said. "What is your plan?"

Mr. Time thought and then said, "I don't want to give him my forgiveness."

"Okay," his father said. "It's your choice, but you can't ask him for his forgiveness in that situation."

Mr. Time was startled. "Why do I need forgiveness from Majeed?"

His father said, "For the reasons Khadija mentioned. That boy needed his father, and you were busy being a father to the world."

Mr. Time confessed, "I just wanted to be like you, Baba."

His father laughed. "You are me, and I am you. You won't truly be successful if you cannot repair the bridge with your son. Do not leave him with hurt in his heart and regret in yours. Fix it."

The sage words licked at the wound that could be healed with kindness. Mr. Time wasn't ready to say the words, let alone ask for the same. He knew his stubbornness would undo him, but he held onto the bitterness because he had lived with it for so long—he didn't know how to let it go.

For the rest of his dream he prayed for guidance.

In the morning light, Khadija and his father's words made sense. He needed to free himself of this negativity to move ahead with his limited life and toward the finality of his death.

He asked the nurse for the phone. She was not used to him making any requests of her, and she was immediately aware of him. She could see that he seemed lively, and she wondered for a moment if he could possibly be getting better. She realized that she would be foolish to believe this, as there was no escape from old age. She had heard voices from his room, and she had been concerned about his mental health for a little while.

She brought him a phone, and he called Majeed.

"*Assalaamalikum, beta,*" Mr. Time greeted Majeed.

"*Walikum salaam, Baba,*" Majeed replied with immediate concern. His father never called.

"Beta, it would be good to see you. Do you have some time today?" Mr. Time made his request.

"Yes, sure. I can be there in an hour," Majeed answered.

Mr. Time prepared to express himself to his son, correct the mistakes of the past, and let go of the mustard seed-sized bitterness in his heart.

Mr. Time cleaned himself up and made sure his son's favorite biscuits were out on a plate. He sat patiently and waited with the remembrance of God on his lips. He wanted to see his Creator and for his Creator to be pleased with him. He was resolute that he must correct all the wrongs in his life with Majeed immediately.

Majeed was a blessing, but also his last test in this life. Mr. Time understood that a test was an opportunity to grow in closeness with his Creator, and Mr. Time wanted to get this right more than anything in his life. Azrael, Khadija, and his Father had all given him fair warning.

His senses sharp, he heard Majeed outside the room speaking to the nurse.

The nurse said to Majeed, "He seems different today, Majeed. There's no easy way to say this, but I would prepare for some sad news soon."

Mr. Time heard snivels as Majeed took the news of his father's health. It occurred to him that his son was also vulnerable, and his fatherly instinct to protect his son swelled in his heart.

After a few deep breaths from Majeed, he said to the nurse, "Yes, I think you are right. I have a strong feeling that he won't be here for long."

The compassion in the nurse shone through as she said, "Make peace with him, and enjoy the time you have together."

Majeed held his tears back. He said, "I love him. It's too hard to think of saying goodbye."

Tears ran down Mr. Time's cheeks. He had never heard his son say that he had loved him. These were words reserved for Khadija—not him.

Light entered his heart, and the burden of bitterness was washed away with every tear. The heaviness was lifted away, and he knew that it was his job to protect his son as long as there was breath left in his body. He realized for the first time in a very long time just how much he loved his son. He forgave him right then.

Mr. Time composed himself and pretended to be asleep when Majeed entered the room. He did not want Majeed to know that he had overheard his conversation with the nurse.

3.5 THE END

"*Assalaamalikum, Baba,*" Majeed said as he customarily checked his father's pulse.

"*Walikum salaam,*" Mr. Time responded, his arms outstretched to embrace his son.

Immediately, the mood was different in the room.

Majeed smiled and said, "You asked me to come, Baba. I came as fast as possible."

"Thank you, Majeed." Mr. Time took a deep breath and began. "I love you. You are my son. You are my progeny, as are your children." The words tumbled out of his mouth with love and affection. He continued, "I am not long for this world, and I will pass soon. Please, forgive me?"

Majeed was in tears again. He had never expected his father to ask for his forgiveness. This act showed him what a great man Mr. Time was. All those years of passive neglect from his father, constantly being passed over, always being compared to other talented brothers and sisters, they all melted away. He saw his father as a statesman and spiritual leader, not a father who nurtured his childish musings. From an early age, he wondered if his father was even aware of his existence.

This magnanimous man was asking for his forgiveness and without a small seed of doubt, he said, "Of course, Baba! Of course, I forgive you. I love you, and there is nothing to forgive."

Past hurt flew out of Majeed's soul like a caged bird set free. Mr. Time felt his pain melt away and his heart soften.

Majeed repeated his request. "Baba, please forgive me? And make your rights on me *halal* and rightful?"

Mr. Time complied and granted them orally in their entirety. For the first time, Mr. Time was free from the prison of his mind, where his culture was his frame of reference. He forgave Majeed for rehousing him in the old people's home.

They hugged and kissed each other with mutual tears, respect, love, and tenderness. Mr. Time contemplated how alike they were. He thought of his father's words telling him that his son was like him. They spoke frankly, and Majeed confessed that his father's achievements had made him feel as if he could never attain what his father had achieved. He felt the need for perfection drove him not to achieve anything, and he decided to have smaller dreams.

Majeed held his hand as he spoke of his family and his life. Mr. Time saw Azrael enter the room.

"You are early. I have another day." Mr. Time spoke to Azrael, but Majeed could not see him.

"Sorry, Baba, who is early?" Majeed asked looking round the empty room trying to see who his father was talking to. Majeed could not see Azrael standing next to him.

Mr. Time's breath became raspy, and his face was panic-stricken as the pangs of death took hold.

Instinctively, Majeed knew that something was wrong. He hit the panic button above his father's bed, and the nurse rushed into the room. A lot of activity ensued. Machines and doctors rushed around as Mr. Time's toes became cold and numb.

The numbness spread quickly up his legs as his soul and his body were separated, artery by artery. The pain was excruciating. Mr. Time could see where Majeed was standing out of the way in the corner of the room. Khadija, his father, and his mother were standing at the end of the bed, calling him into what looked like a garden with beautiful flowers and a clear blue sky filled with birds.

Majeed was crying, and Mr. Time looked at him. It was the final look to say goodbye. Majeed understood, and he launched into the last piece of service he could offer his father. It was the greatest gift that Majeed could give. Majeed recited *Surah Yaseen* from the Qur'an—the very heart of the Qur'an. Mr. Time smiled at him as he mustered his last *shahada* (Islamic testimony of belief), an acknowledgment that he was grateful to Majeed for this last service.

It took over a minute for Azrael to remove Mr. Time's soul from his body—a minute of what felt like being stabbed by three hundred swords simultaneously. The pain of death was the worst pain he had ever experienced, and he would take the memory of the pain with him into the afterlife. The pain came from the physical pain of separation and the emotional pain of leaving his limbs and his life.

He looked at his family as visions of his past flashed before his eyes. He had more of the good stuff than the bad, and because of his unwavering belief in his Creator, he had confirmation that he was destined for Heaven, which was a relief and the best accomplishment he could have ever achieved.

As Majeed cried, Khadija and Mr. Time embraced. This time, he could feel her fully against him. It was a tear-filled reunion, and he greeted his father and mother. Everyone he had loved would be with him soon, and his soul felt reinvigorated.

Mr. Time turned to Azrael, who stood watching the scene. "Why did you come early? I thought I had more time."

Azrael said, "When you asked your son for forgiveness first, your scroll was corrected. Your Creator knew you could be humble, and this is a quality he loves."

Mr. Time understood that the humble man was the man who attracted mercy.

Majeed cried as he looked at his father's lifeless body with its dry lips and open eyes, and he knew his father had been speaking with another being inside the room just before passing on. After death, his father's face had settled into a serene and thoughtful pose. He hoped with all his might that his father would not face the torment of hellfire.

There was a rawness of emotion in loss and death, as if every nerve ending was exposed to the elements. He hoped he would see his father again in his dreams first and then in his afterlife. He recited the creed of belief of a Muslim, and in years to come, he would be grateful that he made peace with his father and that his father had not died alone. In time, he felt honored that he was with him, and he couldn't shake the feeling that his father might have known what would happen. He was grateful that he went to his father and shared those last precious moment with him. It made the healing process easier.

Majeed spent years giving money to charity in his father's name, hoping to benefit his father in his afterlife, and he even completed a pilgrimage in his father's name. He wished he had known his father better, but he was still grateful for the time they spent together that afternoon.

He only had best wishes for his father, and he hoped that he would have a similar death.

When his father appeared in his dreams, he knew this was a request for Majeed to pray for him, and Majeed took his father's example and prayed for his father and his own end.

4 ABOUT THE AUTHOR

Ayse Hafiza is a Londoner born and bred. Her family history is full of authors, so her destiny was predetermined. As a child, her doting father read bedtime stories that included colorful tales of sultans, emirs, maharajas, and maharanis. Daytime was reserved for stories of prophecy, and the mystical world of the Jinn. The result was a rich tapestry of stories that fueled her imagination from an early age.

The youngest child of immigrant parents, education, profession, and professionalism were highly valued for both genders.

After finishing university, she had an illustrious career in the commercial world, employed in sales and business development roles by leading global technology brands. Her work often involved business trips all around the world.

It was during a secondment in Singapore that she connected with her spiritual self, which resulted in her completing *Hajj* (pilgrimage) at an early age. Later, she was guided to Sufic study circles, which she attended for many years.

After falling in love and marrying, she moved to Istanbul and now regularly travels between the two historic and beautiful cities of London and Istanbul.

She has produced two series of short stories, is cooperating on a joint novel, and has previously written screenplays.

5 ADDITIONAL TITLES FROM AYSE HAFIZA

Jinn Series - Expected to be published in 2016

Possessing Asya
The Crush
Magician's Assistant
Devil's Daughter
The Egyptologist
Confessions of a Witch

The Jinn Series involves the mystical Jinn beings, who lived on Earth before us and live in a parallel dimension to mankind. The Jinn are mentioned in the Qur'an, and originate from smokeless fire, whereas mankind was made of clay. The Jinn possess supernatural capabilities.

Each story is unique and a work of dark fiction, and inspired by:

Surat - Al Jinn, Holy Qur'an
Scholastic understanding of Jinn
Cultural stories told
Real world events

6 DISCLAIMER

All characters in this book have no existence outside the imagination of the author and have no relationship whatsoever to anyone bearing the same name or names. This story was not inspired by any individuals known or unknown to the author. Any resemblance of any character to real persons, alive or dead, is purely coincidental.

Additionally, the author claims to have no knowledge of the afterlife and or any of the angels or mystical beings covered in the contents of this story.

The content of this story is the result of the author's private study of scholarly and fictional literature. It is only the author's imagination, perspective, and limited understanding that is represented by this fictitious series of short stories.

The author wants to convey expressly she has no connection with any religious or political body of thought, group, organization, or otherwise.

In short, her works are only her own.

Made in the USA
Charleston, SC
30 May 2016